Praise for the Chocoholic Mysteries

The Chocolate Bridal Bash

"Entertaining and stylish. . . . Reading this on an empty stomach is hazardous to the waistline because the chocolate descriptions are . . . sensuously enticing. Lee is very likable without being too sweet."
—*Midwest Book Review*

"The sixth delicious mix of chocolate and crime."
—Writerspace

"JoAnna Carl's books are delicious treats, from the characters to the snippets of chocolate trivia . . . fantastic characters who have come to feel like good friends. *The Chocolate Bridal Bash* stands alone, but once you've read it, you'll be craving the other books in this series."   —Roundtable Reviews

The Chocolate Mouse Trap

"A fine tale."   —*Midwest Book Review*

"I've been a huge fan of the Chocoholic Mystery series from the start. I adore the mix of romance, mystery, and trivia . . . satisfying."
—Roundtable Reviews

continued . . .

The Chocolate Puppy Puzzle

"The pacing is perfect for the small-town setting, and the various secondary characters add variety and interest. Readers may find themselves craving chocolate, yearning to make their own. . . . An interesting mystery, fun characters, and, of course, chocolate make this a fun read for fans of mysteries and chocolates alike."   —The Romance Readers Connection

The Chocolate Frog Frame-Up

"A JoAnna Carl mystery will be a winner. The trivia and vivid descriptions of the luscious confections are enough to make you hunger for more!"
                                    —Roundtable Reviews

"A fast-paced, light read, full of chocolate facts and delectable treats. Lee is an endearing heroine. . . . Readers will enjoy the time they spend with Lee and Joe in Warner Pier, and will look forward to returning for more murder dipped in chocolate."
                                    —The Mystery Reader

The Chocolate Bear Burglary

Descriptions of exotic chocolate will have you running out to buy gourmet sweets. . . . A delectable treat."
                                    —The Best Reviews

The Chocolate Jewel Case

A Chocoholic Mystery

JoAnna Carl

A SIGNET BOOK

SIGNET
Published by New American Library, a division of
Penguin Group (USA) Inc., 375 Hudson Street,
New York, New York 10014, USA
Penguin Group (Canada), 90 Eglinton Avenue East, Suite 700, Toronto,
Ontario M4P 2Y3, Canada (a division of Pearson Penguin Canada Inc.)
Penguin Books Ltd., 80 Strand, London WC2R 0RL, England
Penguin Ireland, 25 St. Stephen's Green, Dublin 2,
Ireland (a division of Penguin Books Ltd.)
Penguin Group (Australia), 250 Camberwell Road, Camberwell, Victoria 3124,
Australia (a division of Pearson Australia Group Pty. Ltd.)
Penguin Books India Pvt. Ltd., 11 Community Centre, Panchsheel Park,
New Delhi - 110 017, India
Penguin Group (NZ), 67 Apollo Drive, Rosedale, North Shore 0745,
Auckland, New Zealand (a division of Pearson New Zealand Ltd.)
Penguin Books (South Africa) (Pty.) Ltd., 24 Sturdee Avenue,
Rosebank, Johannesburg 2196, South Africa

Penguin Books Ltd., Registered Offices:
80 Strand, London WC2R 0RL, England

First published by Signet, an imprint of New American Library,
a division of Penguin Group (USA) Inc.

First Printing, August 2007
10 9 8 7 6 5 4 3 2 1

*For Janet McGee,
without whom I can't cook anything,
sew anything, or watch a bird.*

Acknowledgments

With thanks to friends, relatives, and complete strangers who generously helped me as I tried to get it right. They include Elizabeth Garber and Betsy Peters, who provided information on chocolate; Tracy Paquin, Susan McDermott, and Dick Trull, Michiganders who answered questions about their native state; Dwight Stodola, Helen Jones, and Alice Mayer, who helped me learn about antique jewelry; Jeff Smith, who gave me tips on property insurance; Kim Kimbrell, who described the process of remodeling; Louisa Halfaker, who suggested stealing antiques; and Jim Avance, a font of knowledge on law enforcement.

Chapter 1

Just when I finally found fifteen minutes for myself, the dead man came to the door.

Not that he looked dead.

In fact, he was lively-looking, tall and thin, with dark hair shot with gray. He was nicely dressed in khakis and a blue polo shirt. Only the scar on his cheek kept him from looking distinguished. Instead it made him look rakish—like a James Bond wannabe who might be a good guy to have on your side in a bar fight. And he was smiling widely enough to display canine teeth, which gave him a wolfish look.

A blue Ford pickup truck was parked behind him in our sandy lane. It was pointed toward Lake Shore Drive, which showed he'd come around from Eighty-eighth Street, driving into our semirural neighborhood by the back road and coming past our neighbors' house. Despite this hint that he knew the territory, the man had proved he was a stranger by coming to the front door; all our friends and relations come in through the kitchen.

He showed up about eleven o'clock on a miserably hot Monday in the second week of July. I wasn't at all happy to hear a knock. For once our five house-guests were all occupied elsewhere at the same time, and I wasn't due at TenHuis Chocolade—where a major chocolate crisis was under way—until one. I had been enjoying having a moment alone.

I peeked through the screen door cautiously. We rarely get salesmen, but I didn't know of anyone else who might come by without phoning ahead. "Yes?"

The man's grin seemed familiar, though I was sure I didn't know him. "Hi. Are you Mrs. Woodyard? Mrs. Joe Woodyard?"

"Yes," I answered confidently, though I'd had that title for less than three months.

"I don't suppose your husband is home."

"I expect him shortly." By that I meant in an hour, but I wasn't going to tell a stranger too much.

"Oh? Should I wait? Or I can come back."

"His schedule is indelicate." Yikes! I'd twisted my tongue in a knot. As usual. "I mean indefinite!" I said. "His schedule is indefinite. Can I give him a message?"

"Well . . ." The stranger sighed deeply, then smiled again, showing those wolfish eyeteeth. "I guess you could tell him his father came by," he said.

I remember staring at him for at least thirty seconds before I answered.

"I'll tell him," I said.

Then I slammed the door. The real, solid door, not the screen door. And I turned the dead bolt above the handle.

I moved away from the door, but the man on the porch was still clearly visible through the window. I knew he could see me too, if he glanced inside. I didn't like that idea, so I went around the fireplace and stood at the bottom of the stairs. This seemed more subtle than slamming our antique casement windows shut and yanking the curtains closed.

Now the stranger couldn't see me lurking behind the fireplace, but I couldn't see him either. And I found that I wanted to keep an eye on him. Where could I hide and watch him?

Hide? Why did I have the impulse to hide? The idea was absurd. Why should the idea of someone claiming to be Joe's father make me look for a closet to duck into?

So I moved out into the living room. I didn't hide, but I did stay near the fireplace, away from the windows, where a person walking casually through the yard wouldn't be able to easily see me. If the man looked in through a window, I decided, I'd call the police.

Of course, if he wanted to get into the house, I had no way of stopping him short of hitting him with the fireplace poker. I had locked the front door, but our house—built in 1904—has no air-conditioning. With the temperature and the humidity both in the nineties, all the windows and doors were open. I might lock the front door, but an intruder could come in any other door or any window without trouble.

The man didn't look into the house. I heard his footsteps leaving the porch, and I heard the door of the pickup open. He was going away. I wondered what Joe would make of the visit when I told him about it.

He might know who the man was, I realized. He might even want to contact the guy.

I grabbed a pen and a piece of junk mail that happened to be lying on the coffee table, rushed to the front door, unlocked it, and ran outside. The truck was just pulling away, and I waved the man down. He opened the right-hand window and leaned across the truck's seat.

I tried to keep my voice noncommittal. "Can you leave a phone number?"

A faint smile crossed the man's face. Again, he seemed familiar, and suddenly I knew why. That grin—the corners of his mouth went up just like Joe's. And his eyes were the same bright blue.

I caught my breath, but I didn't speak.

The stranger put the truck in gear. "I'm not sure where I'll be," he said. "I'll call later."

He drove away, and I stood there gaping after him.

He simply could not be Joe's dad.

Only a few weeks earlier, I had laid a wreath of plastic carnations on Andrew Joseph Woodyard's grave. Joe's dad had been dead for nearly thirty years.

Chapter 2

As soon as the truck had turned onto Lake Shore Drive, I dashed for the phone to call Joe. But my plan followed the pattern our whole summer was taking—it didn't work out. The line at Joe's boat shop was busy on my first try, and before I could hit redial, three of our houseguests showed up.

First the white pickup with the camper pulled in and parked beside the garage. Darrell Davis got out, studiously ignoring me as I waved at him through the kitchen window. He walked around to the back of the truck, shoulders slumped in his usual sullen posture, and climbed into the camper. At least Darrell had his own bed. He didn't sleep in the house, and he had a portable potty. He dumped the potty and showered at the boat shop, although he ate with us. So he wasn't exactly a houseguest. A yard guest, I suppose. He got power for his lamp and his fan from our garage.

Darrell was Joe's guest, if we had to choose sides. Joe had dropped out of the full-time practice of law five years earlier to restore antique motorboats and work part-time as Warner Pier City Attorney. But for several years just after law school, he'd been with a

Legal Aid–type agency in Detroit. Darrell, back when he was eighteen, had been one of Joe's clients. He'd been accused of a home invasion—one that resulted in the death of a notorious drug dealer. Joe had been convinced Darrell was innocent of the killing, but Darrell had been convicted anyway. He'd gone to prison. Joe and some of his investigator pals had hung in there, and five years later another guy had confessed to the crime. Darrell was released without a stain on his character. Unless you count the trauma of five years in prison.

Joe had heard that Darrell had completed a carpentry course but couldn't get a job. The next thing I knew, Darrell had been hired for the summer to help Joe with a remodeling project at our house and to be an extra pair of hands at the boat shop. I'd also come up with some work we needed for TenHuis Chocolade, installing shelves in a storeroom, and Darrell had promised to work that in. Joe couldn't afford to pay Darrell much, so meals and a parking place for his camper were part of the deal.

Did I trust Joe's belief in Darrell? Yes. Did I like having a guy who had spent five years behind bars living in my backyard? No.

The five-year-old Ford driven by Brenda, my stepsister, pulled in and parked in the drive. Her passenger was Tracy Roderick, who had morphed into a houseguest a few days earlier. Both of them were working the retail counter at TenHuis Chocolade that summer, and Brenda was staying with us. Tracy was a guest for the rest of July, while her parents drove across Canada.

The two girls got out of the car carrying shopping bags, their eighteen-year-old jaws spewing conversation.

When I'd first met Tracy, she'd barely turned sixteen, and she was mainly identified by stringy, dirty blond hair. But during the past two years Tracy had grown up. She was much more poised, and she had developed a nice figure. A good haircut and a few highlights had made her hair a shiny, tawny blond. If Tracy had a character flaw, it was one that most of us have: She loved to gossip. But all in all, she had become an attractive and responsible young woman.

I was counting on that responsibility to rein in Brenda. I'd been seventeen when I acquired a stepmother and a five-year-old stepsister. Now, thirteen years later, Brenda and I had never lived in the same household for more than three months, so we barely knew each other. We'd never had any opportunity—or any particular reason—to become more than acquaintances.

But Brenda, along with my dad and her mom, had come to Warner Pier when Joe and I got married three months earlier, and Brenda guarded the guest book at the reception. Tracy was serving cake, so the two of them met, and Tracy introduced Brenda to the college-age crowd of Warner Pier. The first result was a long-distance romance for Brenda with a guy named Will VanKlompen. The second result was Brenda's application for a summer job at TenHuis Chocolade. It's hard to turn your stepsister down. Brenda would be staying with us until mid-August.

Although Brenda used my maiden name, McKinney, no one would take us for sisters. Brenda was around five-four—not a nearly six-foot giraffe like me. And she had dark hair and eyes and a smooth olive complexion, again contrasting with the blond hair I owe to the TenHuis genes my mother passed on and the greenish hazel eyes I got from the Texas side of my family. Her figure was curvy and cute, and she had dimples. I could see why a guy like Will, who had grown up taking west Michigan's tall Dutch blondes for granted, would be bowled over by her.

Both Brenda and Tracy were wearing tank tops over shorts tight enough to show off their fannies.

"Hi, Lee," Brenda said. "I found a really cute bathing suit."

"Yeah," Tracy said. "Now if it'll just stay warm enough to wear it."

Brenda laughed. "It's sure hot enough today! I can't believe y'all don't have air-conditioning up here. And the ones who have it run it with the windows open!"

"In Michigan we don't need air-conditioning all that often," Tracy said. "At least, that's what my mom says."

"That's what Aunt Nettie says, too," I said. "Personally, I think you should have air-conditioning even if you need it only an hour a year. But the picturesque casement windows in this house make it complicated to install window units, and Joe says we need a second bathroom more than we need central air. Maybe next year we'll get it. Until then we'll all swelter together."

"Oh, the heat will break soon," Tracy said. "It never lasts very long." She sounded more confident than I felt. We were moving into our fifth day of miserable heat and humidity, and the TV weather forecast wasn't hopeful.

The girls went upstairs, still chattering, and I reached for the phone again. Then I heard a timid knock at the screen door.

"Mrs. Woodyard?" Darrell always spoke softly. I could barely hear him.

I opened the door. "Hi, Darrell," I said, maybe acting a little friendlier than I felt. "And please call me Lee."

Darrell ducked his head. He was tall, but managed to bend his spine into a shape that took six inches off his height. He pulled the ball cap off his wispy, light brown hair. The effect was that he was bowing and touching his forelock, like the undergardener in a British period novel.

When he spoke again, his voice was still soft. "Sure, Lee. Joe said to tell you he won't get home for lunch. Some guy showed up with a fancy boat he wants restored. He asked Joe to go eat with him."

"Oh." That meant I'd have to wait to talk to Joe about the stranger who'd claimed to be his dad. "It's a little early for lunch, Darrell, but are you ready for a sandwich?"

"I don't want to bother you, Mrs. Woodyard."

"That was the deal. You help Joe, and we feed you. So if you're hungry, come on in. Or you can wait until straight-up noon. You're not getting anything fancy either time."

"Now's fine," Darrell said. "I can wait in the camper."

"Aw, come on in and talk to me. How'd your morning go?"

"Okay." Darrell sidled into the house and stood in the doorway between the kitchen and the dining room. "Joe taught me to operate his paint sprayer."

"Now that you can do that, you'll get stuck with a lot of spraying," I said. "That's not Joe's favorite job." I got a stack of paper plates, a handful of paper napkins, and a bag of potato chips from the back hall, which we use as a pantry. Darrell moved to let me into the dining room, and I put them on the table, which we keep covered with washable vinyl.

"Would you mind opening these chips, Darrell? I think we can just eat them out of the sack. I told you lunch wasn't going to be fancy."

Darrell expertly pulled the top of the chip bag apart.

Before I could turn back to the kitchen, I heard Brenda tripping downstairs. Literally. She couldn't seem to get the hang of the narrow turn at the landing, but so far she hadn't fallen all the way down.

There were a couple of soft thuds as she caught herself, then rapid thuds as she ran on downstairs. There was a loud thump as she reached the living room, right around the corner from where Darrell and I were standing in the dining room. Before I could say anything, Brenda spoke.

"What do you think? Are the polka dots too much?" She swung into the room, putting a hand on the frame of the open French doors between the living and dining rooms. She pivoted into a sexy pose. She was wearing an extremely skimpy bikini.

She and Darrell saw each other at the same moment.

All I heard was two startled gasps. Then I was alone in the dining room while Brenda's feet thudded back up the stairs, and the back door slammed behind Darrell.

"Damn," I said calmly.

The summer was sure getting interesting.

I yelled out the back door, "I'll call you when lunch is ready!" Then I followed Brenda up the stairs. I found her in my old bedroom, which she and Tracy were sharing. Brenda was standing in the corner, her eyes the size of Frisbees, while Tracy lay on the bed, laughing hysterically.

"Brenda, if you wear that bikini at the Warner Pier Beach," I said, "guys are going to look at you."

Brenda's mouth got straight and firm. "Maybe they'd be guys I *wanted* to look at me. Why didn't you tell me Darrell was down there?"

"I thought you would hear us talking."

"He always whispers! That's one of the creepy things about him."

Tracy sat up. "What's with that guy?"

"Darrell? He's a former client of Joe's. Joe thinks he's a good worker."

"People around town are saying—"

"Tracy!" I deliberately made my voice sharp. "When you asked if you could stay here for a month, what did I tell you?"

Her lips got as tight as Brenda's. "No gossip."

"Right. And I'm going to hold you to it. Remember. . ."

"I know, I know." She went on in a singsong voice. "Large-minded people talk about ideas; ordinary people talk about things; small-minded people talk about other people."

"Yes," I said, "and you're too kind a person to be small-minded."

Brenda pouted. "Are you going to try to improve my character, too?"

"Nope. When I told your mom you could come for the summer, I said I was going to be neither a mother nor a chaperone. You're in charge of your own character."

I turned toward the stairs. "I'm going to get all the sandwich stuff out, but I have to be at work at one, so I'll be leaving the dirty dishes for you two. But we're using paper plates. I'll call when everything's on the table."

I paused at the door. "And Brenda, the swimming suit looks fine, but before you wear it to Warner Pier Beach you might want to get a bikini wax."

I plodded downstairs, ready to get out the cheese, lunch meat, and bread. And chocolates for dessert— TenHuis chocolates, which the heat was forcing me to keep in the refrigerator. Aunt Nettie would be horrified. Chocolates should not be refrigerated, but when the truffles were going to melt into puddles, I didn't have much choice.

The summer was becoming stranger and stranger. I guess that a ghost in a blue pickup shouldn't have surprised me; I'd already had enough surprises to last the whole season.

Joe and I had looked forward to having a summer when we could concentrate on each other, on becoming a married couple.

Instead, two things had happened. Good things, in the main, but they distracted us from each other.

Since I'd come to Warner Pier two years earlier to become business manager for my aunt's chocolate company, I'd lived with her in the 1904 house on Lake Shore Drive. The house was basically a small Midwestern farmhouse. It had been built by my great-grandfather, a furniture maker in Grand Rapids, who used it as a summer cottage for his family. When my grandfather, Henry TenHuis, came back from World War II, he'd winterized the cottage to use it as a year-round home. He married my grandmother, built a service station and garage in Warner Pier, and raised my mom and my uncle Phil in the house. He died when my mom was a senior in high school. My grandmother continued to live in the house until she died a few years later, and Uncle Phil and Aunt Nettie had moved in thirty years ago.

I wasn't too surprised that Aunt Nettie decided I should have the house. She'd lived there for much of her married life, true, but she always described herself as "a TenHuis in-law." I was the last actual "TenHuis descendant," she'd told me. I'd assumed that I'd get the property at some indefinite future time when Aunt Nettie, God forbid, couldn't live on her own.

Aunt Nettie was a lively and energetic lady who was barely past sixty. She wasn't even talking about retiring. I had thought of the day when she'd give up her home as far away.

But when Joe and I got married, her wedding present to us was a deed to the property. We were astonished. We weren't quite so astonished to learn the reason: she was planning to remarry.

For a year Aunt Nettie had been keeping company with Warner Pier's police chief, a tall guy who looks like Abraham Lincoln. The single women of Aunt Nettie's generation considered Hogan Jones the best catch in Warner Pier. He could have taken up with women wealthier—and yes, with women more attractive—than my plump aunt Nettie. But he'd chosen her. I considered their romance a tribute to Aunt Nettie's disposition and Hogan's insight into human nature. I expected them to be very happy.

While Joe and I were in New York on our honeymoon, Aunt Nettie and Hogan slipped away and got married at the Warner County courthouse. Then Aunt Nettie began living at Hogan's house, and she handed us the TenHuis family property. Joe was able to get out of the lease on his apartment, and it seemed foolish not to move right into the old house, even though we had to act in a hurry.

Aunt Nettie and Hogan were spending the month of July abroad, first on a barge cruising the rivers of Germany and then visiting Aunt Nettie's friends in the Netherlands, where she'd spent a year learning to make those fantastic truffles and bonbons that TenHuis Chocolade's promotional literature describes as "handmade chocolates in the European tradition."

Aunt Nettie hadn't really moved out completely when she and Hogan left for Europe, so the house was still full of her furniture. Joe and I put most of our own stuff—including around a hundred wedding presents—in the garage. But basically we had two housefuls of furniture and would until Aunt Nettie and Hogan got back and sorted things out.

Joe decided that—since things were confused anyway—we might as well remodel. We would put in that upstairs bathroom Aunt Nettie had always intended to add. And while we were at it, we could extend the kitchen to add room for a dishwasher and could push the downstairs bathroom's wall out to accommodate a stall shower.

Joe loves working with his hands, so my suggestion that we find a contractor was ignored. Joe hired Darrell and started digging holes for the new foundation. At least he wasn't putting a basement under the addition.

Then more people who needed room and board began showing up.

Joe and I were getting used to being a married couple in a situation that included a construction project and five houseguests.

Each houseguest had a different schedule for meals and laundry and going to bed and getting up. There were five vehicles—luckily two of our guests were afoot—trying to share a driveway that will hold three cars only if they're parked at exactly the right angle. People were raiding the refrigerator. People were wanting to watch different television programs and listen to different radio stations. Plus we had only one bathroom, and that was about to lose one of its walls.

And now Brenda didn't want Darrell looking at her in her new bikini.

I had almost decided to run away from home when I heard the clippity-clop of high heels on the stairs. Joe's aunt Gina was coming down.

I groaned. At least Darrell wasn't intrusive, and I liked Brenda and Tracy. But Gina seemed to intrude everywhere, and I didn't like her.

But maybe, I thought, she'd know something about the stranger who had claimed to be Joe's father. After all, Gina was his sister.

Chapter 3

I listened as Gina carefully picked her way down our wooden stairs. If she wouldn't insist on wearing high-heeled shoes, she could walk downstairs without doing that teeter-totter act, I thought angrily. And why did she have to dye her hair that awful lifeless black? And why did she wear those skinny leggings that made her legs look like sticks, and those big bright tunics that made her body look as round as a beach ball? And why did she pile on that clunky junky jewelry? And why did she call me "hon" when I don't even like her?

And why did she knock every single drop of Christian charity out of my mind and spirit?

I'd had a good upbringing mainly because of my Texas grandmother, Rose McKinney, who babysat for me most of my childhood. When I was critical of people, Grandma Rose would always say, "Have a little Christian charity, Lee. Try to understand other people's problems."

So before Gina appeared in the dining room doorway I reminded myself that Joe's aunt had had a lot of problems and deserved pity, not resentment. I

looked at her and accepted the dead black hair, the
kelly green tunic, the red beads, the long red earrings,
and the glittery cardinal pinned on her shoulder. Then
she spoke—"Hi, hon"—and knocked every charitable
thought out of my mind.

I hope I kept my feelings out of my voice as I
greeted her. "Hi, Gina. Did you finish your book?"

"Yes, I did, hon. You wouldn't have time to stop
at the library for me this afternoon, would you?"

"I don't leave the shop until after nine o'clock, but
I might be able to do it before I go in."

"Oh, hon, I don't want to be a bother."

But you are *a bother,* I thought. Out loud I said,
"Lunch is nearly ready."

"Good." Gina started toward the back hall, where
the bathroom is located. "But first I must use the . . ."
She frowned. "Are the facilities in use?"

"Not unless somebody snuck around through the
bedroom."

Gina went past me, and I heard the bathroom door
close. I hoped she wouldn't stay in there teasing that
awful hair too long. I was determined to ask her about
Joe's dad's death. But was the information I might get
worth the strain of trying to dig it out of Gina?

I didn't have the slightest idea what Gina was doing
in my house anyway.

I'd met Gina before Joe and I were married, of
course, and she'd brought Joe's grandmother to our
wedding. Gina—short for Regina—lived in a small
town in central Michigan, where she ran what was
reported to be a successful antique shop. Joe's ninety-
one-year-old grandmother had an apartment in a retirement center in the same town. As her mother's
only surviving child, Gina was the "designated daughter," and by all reports, she visited her mother several times weekly, took her on excursions, shopped

for her, escorted her to doctor's appointments, and handled all the other details of caring for an elderly parent. Grandma Ida was not particularly incapacitated, considering her age, but she needed a family member to help her out now and then.

I'd never heard Gina complain about taking responsibility for her mother. So Gina had her good points, even if she did call me "hon."

But I couldn't understand why she was at my house instead of halfway across Michigan running her business and taking care of her mother. A week earlier, Gina had shown up and announced that she wanted to pay us a short visit. When Joe pressed her for a reason, she said she was getting a divorce—Joe said he thought it was her fifth—and her ex-husband was making things "unpleasant." She was vague about what "unpleasant" episodes had occurred. Gina denied that her ex had threatened or physically abused her—reasons that would have made it evident why she needed to hide out.

Because hiding out was exactly what Gina was doing. She had stashed her car someplace in Holland, and she never left the house.

Not that she spent a lot of time with the rest of us. Most of the time she was upstairs, lying on the double bed that took up most of the floor space in our smallest bedroom, reading, while a box fan blew the damp air over her. She had read at least twenty romance novels in the week she'd been a houseguest. She came down only to use the bathroom.

And to eat. Gina never missed a meal, but she always disappeared back upstairs before it was time to do the dishes.

Brenda and Tracy called Darrell "the creeper," and Gina "the dinner guest."

I didn't feel that I could kick Joe's aunt out, and I

thought Joe should be responsible for quizzing her about why she was at our house. But as I opened a package of braunschweiger, I vowed that Gina wasn't going to escape my questions about Joe's dad. I wanted to understand who the stranger who had come to the door was, and learning about Joe's dad—even if he'd been dead for nearly thirty years—might give me a clue.

As Gina drifted back into the kitchen, I pounced. "Gina, tell me about Joe's dad."

"Andy was my big brother. Ten years older than I was."

Joe's grandmother had told me they were only four years apart, but I didn't argue. "Exactly what happened to him?"

"He was drowned. Didn't Joe tell you?"

"Joe was only five when he died. He doesn't really know a lot about the circumstances, and I hated to ask his mom." Mercy Woodyard runs an insurance agency in Warner Pier.

"How did Joe's dad come to drown?" I asked.

"He was on the crew of a Great Lakes freighter. The ship sank in Lake Superior. It was very tragic. Twenty men were lost."

My heart sank as I considered the possibility that Joe's dad's body had never been found. Surely there was no chance that Andrew Joseph Woodward was still alive.

I tried again. "Joe and I took your mother to the cemetery to put a wreck—I mean, a wreath! Grandma Ida put a wreath on his grave on Memorial Day."

"Yes, Mom's such a darling. She keeps all the old traditions."

"So his body was recovered?"

Gina nodded. "Oh, yes, hon. Mercy went up to Houghton to identify him. It was awful for her."

Was there any way to be tactful about asking how the body was identified? I had to try. "Had he been in the water long?"

"Just a couple of days. Mom insisted we have an open-casket service." Gina frowned. "Why do you want to know all this, hon?"

Should I tell her about the stranger who came to the door? No, I decided. I'd ask Joe about him first.

"I was just curious," I said. "Nobody ever talks about him. Does Joe look like him?"

"Not a lot. Andy wasn't as tall as Joe is, and his hair was lighter. Medium brown, not dark like Joe's. Joe gets his dark hair from Mercy. Her hair was almost black before she decided to go blond. But Joe's face is shaped like Andy's was, and Andy had blue eyes, too." She turned toward the living room, tossing her final comment back over her shoulder. "Joe's smile is a lot like Andy's."

Her words made my stomach do a somersault. It was the stranger's smile that had reminded me of Joe.

I forced myself to act calm. I picked up the platter of cold cuts in one hand and a bowl of lettuce in the other. I'd just turned toward the dining room when the phone rang.

Gina was standing right beside it, and she jumped about a foot off the floor. Her face became a picture of terror.

"Oh, honey!" she said. "That startled me."

She didn't look startled. She looked terrified. I stared at her, trying to understand why an ordinary noise like a telephone would frighten her.

The phone rang again. I gestured with the cold cuts and lettuce, pointing out that my hands were full. "Would you mind getting that, Gina?"

"No, no! Lee, honey, I can't answer the phone! No one must know I'm here."

I turned around and put the cold cuts and lettuce down on the cabinet. I tried not to glare at Gina as I picked up the phone.

"Lee, is that you?"

I recognized the rather creaky voice of Joe's grandmother, so I turned toward Gina, ready to hand her the phone. "Hello, Grandma Ida. How are you?"

Gina's reaction was so unexpected that I missed Grandma Ida's next remark.

Gina shook her head vigorously. "No! No!" she whispered. "Don't tell her I'm here!" Then she ran out of the kitchen. Her high heels went up the stairs with a fast *clomp-clomp.*

"I'm sorry, Grandma Ida," I said. "I didn't hear what you said. Something wrong with the line, I guess."

"I said, have you heard from Regina?"

Should I lie for Gina? Or make her talk to her mother? I had less than a second to make up my mind. I took the coward's way out and asked a new question instead of answering the old one. "Was she going to call us?"

"She's gone someplace, and she didn't tell me where. I was hoping she let somebody in the family know where she is."

"I'm sorry, Grandma Ida. I can't help you. Do you have a product? I mean, do you have a problem?"

"Oh, no, Lee. Things are fine. It just made me nervous—Regina taking off like that. If you hear from her, let me know."

"I'll tell you anything I can," I said, hating myself some and hating Gina a lot.

Grandma Ida and I talked a few more minutes. I told her Joe was busy, but fine, and that married life was great. I didn't mention that it was also crowded and completely lacking in privacy. I'm not sure my comments made much sense. I was racking my brain for an explanation of why Gina would turn her back on her life as a dutiful daughter and refuse even to talk to her mother.

As soon as I hung up, I started for the stairs. But the mantel clock in the living room read twelve.

I groaned. I had only forty minutes before I had to leave for TenHuis Chocolade, and if I was going to stop for Gina's library books, I had only thirty minutes. I plunked the cold cuts and lettuce in the middle of the table, and then grabbed a package of cookies and a box of TenHuis chocolates and put them out. The group would simply have to settle for an indoor, build-your-own-sandwich picnic.

I turned on the column fan we keep in the dining room, went to the back door and yelled, "Darrell!" right into the face of our fifth houseguest.

Pete Falconer had appeared on the back porch like a bird suddenly swooping down from one of the hundred-foot tall maples that surround the house. I hadn't heard his SUV pull in.

I guessed Pete's age as around forty, but he had thick, shiny, prematurely gray hair. The sun was making that hair glint almost white, and his shiny black eyes sent out piercing rays from either side of his generous aquiline nose. Yes, his nose looked like an eagle's beak. Add the broad shoulders and the arms always held slightly flexed from his sides, and Pete became "Eagleman." He'd have been a perfect model for a flying superhero, in case some comic strip artist wanted to base one on a bird. Pete might not have feathers, but he always looked as if he were ready to take off into the stratosphere.

Which was a silly idea, I reminded myself. A six-foot-five-inch guy carrying over two hundred pounds of solid muscle would be too heavy to fly unless he were equipped with a jet engine. All Pete had was an olive green bush hat.

"Whoops!" I said. "Sorry I yelled right in your face, Pete. I didn't see your comet. I mean, coming! I didn't see you coming."

Pete got that sly smile that my slips of the tongue always give him, and I mentally cursed myself. "You're just in time for lunch," I said.

"Great," Pete said. He gestured toward the back hall. "Is it primping time for the little ladies?"

"The bathroom is free."

He went past me, throwing off sparks of testosterone.

Brenda and Tracy have a nickname for Pete, as well as for Darrell and Aunt Gina. To them he's "Mr. Macho." My nickname for him, one I'd never say out loud, is "Pete the Pig." Pig as in male chauvinist pig. The way he'd asked about the girls and the bathroom was typical. He could have said, "Is the bathroom in use?" But no, he used the question to create a picture of "little ladies" selfishly occupying the bathroom.

I could see Darrell climbing out the back of his camper, so I called upstairs to alert Brenda, Tracy, and Gina. Then I went to the table, sat down at one end, and began to make myself a sandwich. I'd promised this bunch food, but they'd have to do without gracious living.

The only thing gracious about the lunch I'd put on the table was the TenHuis chocolates—six Mocha Pyramids ("Milky coffee interior in a dark chocolate pyramid"), five Raspberry Creams ("Red raspberry puree in a white chocolate cream interior, coated in dark chocolate"), and a dozen pieces of molded chocolate. The molded chocolates were from Aunt Nettie's summer special. She was following the theme of jewels, and each tablet of chocolate was embellished with a representation of a piece of jewelry: a string of pearls in white chocolate, a diamond ring in milk chocolate, a dark chocolate spray of flowers representing a Victorian brooch. Each piece was wrapped in jewel-toned foils—silver, gold, ruby red, sapphire blue, or emerald green.

The chocolate jewels we sold at the shop could be bought in boxes also made of chocolate, but the ones I'd put on the table were in a regular white cardboard box with the TenHuis logo on top. All these chocolates were seconds. Because of our heat wave and the shop's air-conditioning problems, they'd developed bloom, a haze of white that strikes horror into the hearts of chocolatiers. But the taste was up to Aunt Nettie's standards, and I hadn't had to pay for them.

Brenda and Tracy thumped down from upstairs. They had put on their brown shirts and khaki Bermuda shorts, the uniform for TenHuis Chocolade counter help. I was wearing my own brown shirt and khaki pants, so we looked like a chorus line.

Gina managed to arrange for her path to intersect with Pete's as he entered from the kitchen. She smiled sweetly, and Pete held her chair and sat beside her.

He preened, and I watched with renewed astonishment.

I don't know how Gina does it. She's somewhere past fifty years old, and her appearance is anything but sexy, but she's still got "it," whatever "it" is. All the men love her. She doesn't even seem to flirt. I don't get it. I especially didn't understand why she wanted to conquer Pete.

Pete and I got off on the wrong foot from the first. I meant to ask him where he and Joe had known each other, and it came out, "Did you meet Joe in detention? I mean, Detroit! Did you know Joe when he worked in Detroit?"

The slip of the tongue had made it obvious that I thought Pete could have been, like Darrell, one of the guys Joe had represented in a criminal case. Pete had laughed at me, and I hadn't been able to say a straight sentence to him since; being nervous makes my speech problem worse.

Then I overheard (there are no secrets in the 1904 house) Pete telling Joe he approved of me. But his opinion wasn't exactly a compliment.

"That first gal you married, she had brains," Pete had said. "This one's gonna believe any damn thing you tell her."

"Don't let Lee fool you," Joe said. "She doesn't miss anything."

"Hey, it's okay!" Pete said. "Every man should marry once for love and once for money. Brains are a side issue." At least he was giving me credit for being Joe's love interest; Joe's first wife was the one with money. But I had disliked Pete from then on.

Darrell came in last, stopping in the dining room doorway and looking around uneasily. "I'll just make a sandwich and take it out to the truck," he said.

Gina patted the chair on the other side of her. "Now, Darrell. You join us."

"Yeah, Darrell," Pete said. "Don't leave me at the mercy of all these pretty girls."

Brenda and Tracy giggled, and Pete winked at them. They giggled harder.

Darrell sat down at the other end of the table and gave a secretive smile. "You can handle them, Pete," he said.

He was right. Pete was the most dangerous kind of male chauvinist pig; the kind women loved. The testosterone I'd caught a whiff of as he went through the kitchen oozed from his pores.

He didn't fit the clichéd picture of a bird-watcher.

But a bird-watcher was what Pete claimed to be and what Joe swore he actually was.

Pete had shown up two days after Gina had, telling Joe he'd just dropped by to say hi and to meet me. He'd been planning to stay near Warner Pier for a week, camping and watching birds, he said, but his camping place had proved to be closed, so he was going back to Detroit. Before I could say, "But we've already got a houseful of people," Joe had said he could stay with us—as long as he didn't mind tossing his sleeping bag on our screened-in porch.

When I got Joe alone, I quizzed him about who Pete was and what he was doing in our house. But Joe had proved uncommunicative. In fact, for the past week I'd barely seen Joe. He was working late at the boat shop, or he'd had to make a quick trip to Lansing on city business, or he'd even spent an evening clo-seted with his mother on some vague family matter neither of them would talk about. Finding time alone with him hadn't been easy, especially when I was doing a lot more cooking than usual, plus the shopping and planning required to feed seven people three meals a day.

I savagely cut my sandwich in half—pretending the slice of braunschweiger on it was a hunk of Joe's hide—and watched as Gina wrapped Pete around her finger and Pete wrapped Gina around his. They were a perfect match: a woman who was a man magnet, and a man women slobbered over. The wonder was that they hadn't hated each other on sight.

Gina was asking Pete about his morning's bird-watching. He replied by producing a digital camera and showing her a picture of an owl. After she'd oohed and aahed, he passed the camera around to the rest of us. And yes, the picture of a great horned owl taking off from a red tile roof was impressive.

Gina moved closer and closer to him, and I got madder and madder. Gina was an independent woman who ran her own business. Why didn't she see Pete the way I did, as the classic male chauvinist?

I realized that Pete and Gina were the only two people having a conversation. Darrell was looking miserable. We'd forced him to join us at the lunch table, but none of us was talking to him.

"Darrell," I said, "Joe says you're really good at carpentry—and you know that's a skill he values highly. How did you learn that?" Then I was afraid I'd asked a tactless question. What if Darrell had learned carpentry in prison?

But he answered in his barely audible voice. "High school vo-tech. I had a good teacher."

A few more questions—about the teacher and the class projects—and Darrell opened up a bit. I could actually hear his voice. Tracy and Brenda talked a little about vo-tech classes in their high schools. Brenda had taken VICA, I learned. Pete and Gina stopped talking only to each other. Pete threw in a funny memory from his own high school shop class.

After twenty minutes of conversation, half a sandwich, a handful of chips, and one Mocha Pyramid, I looked at my watch. "I've got to run," I said. "Gina, if I stop at the library, do you want more of the same?"

Gina loved the "innocent" romances. I thought they were all alike and all nauseating. "Each to his own taste, as the old lady said when she kissed the cow." That was another of my grandmother's sayings.

"Oh, thanks, hon." Gina jumped to her feet. "I'll get the books that are ready to go back."

"I'll just check the mail," I said. "Then I'm leaving. Tracy and Brenda, you're putting up the leftovers and doing dishes, right? And Joe's responsible for dinner."

The girls nodded, mouths full. I went out the front

door and down the sandy drive to the mailbox. I gathered up a handful of junk mail and was looking it over as I came back. When I reached the front walk, I realized that Pete was in the screened-in section of the porch, the section where his sleeping bag and his canvas carryall were stowed, kneeling beside his belongings.

I stepped onto the porch, still looking at the mail in my hand. The Democratic National Committee? How did I get on that mailing list? I studied the envelope. Then I looked up.

I found myself staring into the screened-in porch, my eyes focused on whatever Pete was doing with his carryall.

It took me a second to realize he was tucking a pistol inside.

Chapter 4

At that moment I was so astonished that I could easily have gasped and fallen into a swoon with the back of my hand to my head, like the heroine of one of Gina's romantic novels. But apparently I didn't. I think I quickly dropped my eyes back to my mail and pretended I hadn't noticed the pistol. I almost acted as if I'd accidentally caught Pete with his pants down and was trying not to embarrass either of us.

I went on into the house, put the mail on the mantelpiece where Joe would see it, took the stack of books from Gina, thanked Brenda and Tracy for cleaning up, and went back out the front door. Joe and I had borrowed extra parking space from the Baileys—they were visiting a new grandchild in California—so my van was in their carport, and I had to walk down a little sandy road that led through a patch of woods to get to my transportation.

Pete was standing on the screened-in porch, holding his binoculars. He looked at me challengingly as I went past. I had decided that I didn't expect Pete to shoot the place up, and I didn't feel that I could question Joe's friend. So I went by him with nothing more to say than, "See you later."

I might not want to talk to Pete, but I sure was piling up things to talk to Joe about—if I ever found him.

As I came out at the Baileys' house, I heard the yip of a dog. Our newish neighbor, Harold Glick, and Alice, his blond mutt, were walking toward me along the Baileys' drive. Harold was leasing Inez Deacon's house, about a quarter of a mile south on Lake Shore Drive. Inez, an old friend of Aunt Nettie's and of mine, was now living in a retirement center, but she wasn't quite ready to sell her house, so her daughter had found her a renter. Harold had moved there in February.

Harold seemed to be a pleasant enough guy. He wasn't old enough for retiree activities, though he didn't work, and he didn't have enough friends and family to keep him occupied. He seemed lonesome, and I tried to be neighborly to him, but he was the most boring man I'd ever met. I guessed his age at around fifty. He was a short scrawny guy with thin gray hair.

He spent a lot of time with Alice. When I got a minute to walk on the beach, it was likely that I'd meet the two of them there, but this was the first time I'd seen him on our road. His presence raised my eyebrows. Our road isn't really public.

The Baileys' drive exits onto Eighty-eighth Street, a side road that turns east off of Lake Shore Drive. The lane we share with the Baileys—as I say, we're in a semirural part of Warner Pier—is actually our drive plus the Baileys' drive linked by an extra bit of sandy roadway Uncle Phil and Charlie Bailey put in. It sometimes makes a convenient way to come and go, in case a truck is blocking one of the driveways, for example. But it's private property, not a Warner Pier street.

Alice barked again, and Harold shushed her. Then he spoke. "Hi, Lee. Is it hot enough for you?"

"Much too hot for me, Harold."

"But you're a Texan. I guess you're used to heat."

"Texas is air-conditioned! We don't put up with this kind of heat without a fight. And we certainly don't try to live with this kind of humidity without doing something about it."

Before I could point out that Harold was on private property, he spoke again. "Did you hear the latest on our crime wave?"

"Another burglary?"

Harold nodded. He'd been hit by burglars the week he moved in, and he took any crime along the lake-shore personally.

"You started quite a fad, Harold. Who's been hit this time?"

"That big white house down by the little cemetery. Terrill? Is that the name?"

"Do you mean Tarleton? There's a gazebo on the lawn? And a sign that says, 'The Lake House'?"

"That's the one. The family came up yesterday for the first time this season and discovered a bunch of stuff missing."

"More antiques?"

Harold shrugged. "I guess so. Were the Tarleton antiques well-known?"

"Not to me. We don't own antiques. Just second-hand furniture." I decided that this was a good moment to point out tactfully that he and Alice were on private property. "Were you coming to see us?"

"No, I'm just trying to get oriented. All these little roads are confusing."

"This drive goes only to our house and the Baileys'. It's not a city street."

Harold smiled an angelic smile. "I didn't mean to trespass, but it's an awfully pleasant walk. Do you mind if Alice and I come through here?"

"I wouldn't do it at night. We might think you were a prowler."

"I wouldn't want Joe to run out with a pistol."

I ignored that. "And watch out for cars. The drives are only one lane wide, as you see, and we have a bunch of people going in and out this year."

Harold nodded. "I walked by yesterday evening and saw that your drive was full. You must have company. Friends or relatives?"

"Some of each." I looked at my watch. "Sorry, Harold, but I'm late to work."

Harold smiled, Alice gave a friendly yip, and the two of them walked on toward our house. I got in my van and drove off.

Harold was okay, but he was nosy as well as boring. I decided that his case of single guy syndrome was getting worse. Maybe Joe could get him to volunteer for some city committee. He might like to clean up the dog-walking area in the Dock Street Park. I snorted at the idea. Harold was none too conscientious about cleaning up after Alice.

And he'd heard of another burglary. There had been a regular string of them along the lakeshore that spring and summer. I'd been too busy getting used to married life to worry about it, but at least a dozen summer cottages had been hit. Like the Tarletons, the owners often hadn't discovered that they had been victims until the cottages were opened for the summer. The main loot had been antiques.

For more than a hundred years, Warner Pier has been populated by three classes of people—locals, tourists, and summer people. Locals, of course, are like Joe and me; we live and work there all the time. Tourists come by car or bus and stay in motels or B and Bs for a weekend, a week, or two weeks. Summer people own cottages or condominiums and stay for a month, two months, or the whole summer.

Lots of the cottages in Warner Pier and along the lakeshore are seventy-five to a hundred years old. Lots of the families have been coming to Warner Pier for seventy-five to a hundred years. Others have built cottages—I'd call some of them mansions—more recently. Some of those cottages have valuable furnishings; some don't. None of us understood how the burglars had managed to hit the ones with valuable antiques every time.

I drove on to the main part of Warner Pier, dashed by the library, tossed Gina's romances into the return slot, and grabbed six more off the romance shelf. She likes the old ones, the ones with innocent heroines and no sex, not the newer ones with independent women and racy scenes.

I went in the back door of TenHuis Chocolade only five minutes late. Ahh, air-conditioning. And ahh, chocolate. I took three deep breaths as I came in the back door. Just sniffing it made me feel better. The ultimate comfort food. And I needed comfort that summer.

But the comfort didn't last long. As I walked into the big, clean kitchen where the fabulous TenHuis chocolates are made, I was confronted with a red-haired giantess looming near the ceiling.

"Oh, no!" Now I realized that the humidity was high, despite the cooler air inside. "Is the air-conditioning out again?"

Dolly Jolly, Aunt Nettie's second in command, was standing on a folding chair and holding her hand in

"You mean the houseguests? Don't worry. I make them wait on themselves."

"No, I meant Joe's mom." Dolly lowered her voice to that low rumble that she thinks is a whisper. "Is she all right?"

"As far as I know. Why?"

Dolly frowned. "Well, she came by, and she looked . . . worried."

"Did she say something was wrong?"

"Not exactly. But she said she wasn't going to re-place her assistant."

"Oh? That is odd. I'll ask her about it."

Joe's mom, Mercy Woodyard, owns Warner Pier's only independent insurance agency. She's probably the most successful businesswoman in Warner Pier—a sit-uation I approve of. Not only do Joe and I not have to worry about her finances, but she keeps so busy at the agency that she rarely bothers us. Mercy could be a formidable force if she decided to mix into our lives. She's so efficient and energetic that she automatically assumes command of most situations.

Mercy runs her office with the help of one assistant, and that assistant had recently announced she and her husband were moving to Lansing. Mercy had been interviewing replacements, but maybe she hadn't been able to find anyone suitable.

Dolly left, and I got busy. TenHuis Chocolade isn't like most Warner Pier businesses—completely depen-dent on the summer tourist season. We ship chocolates to department stores, specialty shops, caterers, and in-dividuals year-round. But summer is still busy for our retail shop as Warner Pier's tourists wander our quaint streets. We have plenty of locals and summer people as customers as well.

I checked in with the two counter girls who would be working until Brenda and Tracy came at four o'clock; then I began on my e-mail. Most of our orders come by e-mail. I have to keep up on it.

I'd finished with the e-mail and moved on to the regular mail by the time young Cal Vandemann came in. I turned him over to Dolly and kept working. Only a few minutes later, Tracy and Brenda came bounding in. I glanced at the clock at the back of the workshop—my office has glass walls, so I can see the retail shop and the workshop. And the clock astonished me. Brenda and Tracy were half an hour early.

Brenda stopped near the door, but Tracy charged right into my office.

"Listen, Lee," she said. "I've got to tell you something."

"What have I done now?"

"You haven't done anything. It's what we heard at the Superette."

"Now, Tracy, if you've been talking to Greg Glossop . . ." Greg Glossop is the pharmacist at Warner Pier's only supermarket, and he's the most notorious gossip in town.

"No! I steered clear of Mr. Gossip, just the way you said I should. But I couldn't help overhearing—"

"Tracy! No gossip!"

"Lee! This is important!"

"Is it true?"

"Of course it's not true!"

"Then I don't want to hear it."

Tracy's face twisted into a knot of agony. "Sometimes gossip can be important, Lee. You need to hear this."

I sighed. "Sit down and tell me. Just don't yell it so the whole shop can hear."

Tracy came in the office, pulled the door shut behind her, and sat in my visitor's chair. She leaned across my desk and dropped her voice.

"Brenda and I were in the cosmetics aisle, see, and you know that's right next to the cereal."

"One aisle over. I know."

"Well, some summer lady was over there. I don't know who she is, but I've seen her in the Superette before. A fake blonde. One of the ones who wears a bikini with a push-up bra."

"In this weather that's a practical garment."

"She didn't have a bikini on today, but I've seen her in one before."

"Okay, Tracy. I get the picture." I began to be afraid the gossip would be that this bikinied blonde was pursuing my husband. I trusted Joe, but I didn't want to hear even an unfounded rumor along those lines. "What did she say?"

"She said that looking for a new insurance agent was such a pain."

"Insurance agent?"

"Yes. Then the woman she was talking to—I looked at her later, and it was some older woman I don't know—that woman said, 'Oh, we've always been happy with Mrs. Woodyard.'"

"I should think so."

"The first woman said, 'Oh, we have, too. Until all these burglaries started.' Then she lowered her voice—you know, the way you do when you're pretending to tell a secret. She dropped her voice, but it was still loud enough for us to hear an aisle over. And she said, 'It just seems awfully funny that only her clients are getting hit in these burglaries. I told Bob we simply can't take the chance of giving a list of our belongings to a thief!'"

For the third time that day, I was completely astonished.

First my dead father-in-law had come to the door. Then I'd discovered that one of my houseguests was packing a pistol. Now I'd been told that my mother-in-law was suspected of being part of a burglary ring.

If I'd had Pete's pistol right at the moment, I might have tracked down the bleached blonde in the bikini with the push-up bra and shot her dead. How dare she say such a thing about Joe's mom? No insurance agent in the world could be more conscientious about guarding the interests of her clients.

Tracy was still looking at me, her eyes wide, eager to see my reaction. I tried to pull myself together and keep my temper. Losing it wouldn't help Joe's mom.

"You were right, Tracy. I did need to hear this," I said. "But no one else does."

Tracy shook her head vigorously. "I won't say a word."

"I guess you and Brenda can talk about it with each other, since she heard it, too. But I'd appreciate your not saying anything to anybody else."

Tracy's head shook so hard she could have scrambled her brain like an omelet.

"Not the boyfriends."

She shook again.

"Not the girlfriends."

Another shake.

"Nobody. In fact, I feel sure that Mercy would have grounds for a lawsuit against anybody who speculated publicly about her professional reputation and behavior. Slander is a serious matter."

Tracy nodded, her eyes bigger than ever.

"I do appreciate your telling me, and I'll talk to Joe about it. Now you and Brenda have time for coffee before you come on duty."

I slipped them each money for a fancy cappuccino and gave Brenda the same caution I'd given Tracy. I hoped the mention of a lawsuit would keep the two of them quiet.

Then I sat down and made a list of the things I needed to talk to Joe about.

His friend Pete's gun. His aunt using our house for a hideout. Our lack of privacy on what was still our honeymoon. This gossip about his mother. And the stranger who claimed to be his father.

What else could come up?

CHOCOLATE BOOKS

Chocolate: A Bittersweet Saga of Dark and Light

by Mort Rosenblum

(NORTH POINT PRESS)

Mort Rosenblum traveled the world to research this book, and it gives a multifaceted look at the wonderful stuff.

For example, some of the growers he observed in Africa dried their cacao beans by spreading them on paved roadways. Another grower, on the island of Principe, had invented elaborate drying machinery. Rosenblum also investigated whether or not African cacao growers are guilty of using slave labor.

Rosenblum visited some modern American makers of fine chocolate, but his book takes its closest looks at European chocolate makers, particularly those in the esoteric world of fine luxury chocolates. Plants and tiny artisan shops that produce elaborate chocolate sculptures and fabulous chocolate creations are described.

Hint: If a maker of fine chocolate offers you a sample of anything in his stock, Rosenblum says to pick a plain dark chocolate. No embellishment. That way you really taste the chocolate.

Chapter 5

When Cal Vandemann reported on the air-conditioning an hour later, the news wasn't good.

"I'm trying not to replace that compressor," he said. "But I'm afraid I have to."

"If we need a compressor, get us one."

"They're really expensive, Lee."

"Not being able to do business is even more expensive, Cal. Get the compressor."

I tried to tell myself Cal couldn't be as dumb as he looked, but his little-kid looks did not encourage confidence. His dad, who had died the previous winter, had been burly. He'd looked like a person who knew air-conditioning. I knew Cal was in his thirties, but he looked like a junior high kid.

Cal scratched his head. "The problem is going to be *finding* a compressor."

"If we need it, we need it, Cal."

"I know, Lee. But it's this heat wave. Everybody else's compressors are out, too."

"Cal, I won't balk at the price." As a business manager, I hated to say that, but we were desperate. "Find one!"

He left. But he didn't look confident.

At least my office was cool. I tried to work, resolutely ignoring the customers and clerks in the shop. I didn't look up when I heard Tracy in an animated conversation with someone, but it didn't save me from interruption. Tracy came to the office door and said, "One of your neighbors wants to talk to you, Lee."

I looked up to see an attractive woman of fifty or so. She was petite and well proportioned and had strawberry blond hair in a fake but tasteful shade. Her coordinated sportswear outfit marked her as a summer person. She looked like the kind of customer who was likely to need a special order—silver trays full of truffles and bonbons, or a hundred souvenir bells for a fiftieth wedding anniversary.

Tracy had said she was a neighbor, but I'd never seen her before. I decided she must be a neighbor from Warner Pier's business district.

She came into my office, and I stood up and tried to look pleasant. "Hi. Are you from the wine shop?"

"Oh, no." The woman smiled. "I'm a neighbor from across Lake Shore Drive. I wanted to introduce myself."

As far as I knew, no one had moved onto Lake Shore Drive since Harold Glick, and I didn't think Harold had a wife. Besides, Harold didn't live *across* the road. He lived *down* the road. So who could this woman be?

I offered to shake hands. "I'm sorry, I didn't realize we had a new neighbor."

"I'm not exactly new. *Re*newed, maybe. I'm Garnet Garrett. We're at the Double Diamond cottage."

"Oh! Please sit down."

Double Diamond was a landmark along the lakeshore, and, yes, it was exactly across Lake Shore Drive from us, although we couldn't see it because of the hundreds of trees between the two houses.

We're on the inland side of the road, but Double Diamond overlooks the lake. I'd seen the cottage from the beach. It was a large, comfortable-looking, Craftsman-style house, with porches on three sides and walls covered with weathered gray shingles. I thought it was surrounded with far too much thick brush, a landscaping style I call "mosquito heaven." But nobody had asked me.

Mrs. Garrett perched on the edge of a chair. "Double Diamond has been leased outside the family for twenty-five years, so I haven't been here since I was a newlywed. But we're planning a family reunion at the cottage later this month."

"I'm originally from Texas," I said, "and when I first saw the cottage's name, I thought a rancher had wandered up here."

She smiled. "The diamonds refer to jewels, not cattle brands. My grandmother was Opal Diamonte."

I'm sure I looked blank, and Mrs. Garrett smiled apologetically. "She was an opera star back in the 1920s."

"Now I remember! Joe's grandmother was thrilled when she came to see us, and learned our house was right across the road from Double Diamond. She's still an opera fan. And wasn't there an exhibit of some of your grandmother's jewelry last winter? I read about it in the Chicago paper."

"Oh, yes, the famous jewels. They're responsible for all our weird family names."

"Garnet? That's not so weird."

"Well, the whole thing is my silly great-grandmother's fault. If she hadn't given her daughter two jewels as a name, we wouldn't be cursed into the third generation."

"Cursed?"

"With crazy names. My grandmother—the opera singer—was named Opal Diamond, if you translate her last name from Italian. She was proud of her name, and she didn't marry until she met a dashing gentleman named Ruben—which means Ruby in German. And his last name was Gold."

We both laughed.

"They thought their names forced them to carry on the jewel tradition. My mother was blessed with Ruby, and her sister with Pearl. And my poor uncle Alex isn't named Alexander. He's Alexandrite."

"A semiprecious stone, right?"

"Right. It has the interesting quality of being green in natural light and red in artificial. That may have marked Uncle Alex's personality, which has always grown more vivid as the sun goes down. Anyway, the family was practically out of jewels by the time my generation appeared. My sister is Jade, and I got Garnet." She smiled again. "I had the bad judgment to add Garrett by falling for a nice guy named Dick Garrett."

I laughed. "I'm afraid to ask if you have children."

"We do. Mary and Richard Junior. Three generations was enough of that jewel nonsense! But my grandmother did have a fabulous collection of Art Deco jewelry, and she supposedly paid for the Warner Pier property—back in 1927—by selling a fancy belt buckle shaped like two linked diamonds and encrusted with diamond stones. Hence the name of the cottage. Everybody thinks we're all rich because of that darn jewelry, but I assure you we're not."

I didn't comment. Lakeshore property near Warner

Pier is so valuable today that a belt buckle would have to contain stones the size of the Hope Diamond to pay for a couple of acres with a view of the water. The Diamonte-Gold descendants might not think of themselves as wealthy, but they owned a nice chunk of real estate.

"I'm afraid I'm not much of a neighbor," I said. "I spend most of my time here at the shop."

"Yes, and you're working right now." Garnet Garrett stood up. "I didn't come in to interrupt you. I simply wanted to say how happy I am that you and your husband are joining us for dinner tomorrow."

Joe and I were having dinner with the Garretts?

I tried to cover my astonishment by ducking my head and looking through the papers on my desk until I found a notepad. And with every second it took me to find it, I pictured Joe roasting over the Garretts' backyard grill. Here we had a regular throng of houseguests to feed and entertain, and he made a social engagement without consulting me? It was definitely an action that merited torture.

By the time I found the notepad, I was—I hoped—in command of my feelings. I smiled at Garnet Garrett. "Let me make a note of the trial. I mean, the time! I'd better write down the time!"

Garnet Garrett smiled sweetly. "Joe hadn't told you, had he?"

I tried to smile back. "I haven't seen him since this morning. He went to lunch with a client from his boat shop."

"That was Dick! My husband. He found my grandfather's old speedboat in a shed, and he couldn't rest until he arranged to have it restored."

"Joe will do a great job, and I'm looking forward to dinner." My smile was making my jaw ache.

The dinner would be strictly informal, Mrs. Garrett

told me. Just five people—the Garretts, Joe and me, and her uncle Alex. We should come at six thirty for drinks on the porch. No, I couldn't bring anything.

I was relieved to hear that. I was scheduled to work from nine to five the next day, and I'd have to feed Gina, Pete, Darrell, Tracy, and Brenda before I could go to the neighbors' house for a relaxing dinner. And Joe was fixing frozen lasagna and bagged salad for the gang at our house today, so I'd have to think of something more creative for the next day. Or at least less Italian. Pizza wouldn't be a good idea.

I said good-bye to Garnet, then pulled out my list of things to talk to Joe about and added to it: *Dinner with Garretts.* I asked Brenda to put a half-pound box of chocolates on my account, so I could take it as a hostess gift. Then I pretended to work.

I hope that I fooled the hairnet ladies, Brenda and Tracy at the counter, and the customers—even the tourists who took a gander at our prices and walked out again. But I couldn't fool myself. Too much had happened that day. My mind was whirling, and I didn't accomplish a thing.

I simply had to talk to Joe, and that wasn't going to be easy.

Our house has a certain rustic charm, but it also has a major problem, and I'm not talking about the excavation for the new bathroom and kitchen foundation. The place is an echo chamber. As a teenager I'd discovered that I could hear anything that went on anyplace in the darn house. Which meant that anybody else in the house could also hear me. The episode when I overheard Pete giving Joe a candid assessment of my mental capacity was typical of how things went in that house.

So even though Joe and I had managed to reserve the use of the one downstairs bedroom just for the two of us, we had to be cautious about talking in there. Between Brenda, Tracy, and Gina overhead and Pete out on the porch—well, we'd spent the past two weeks learning to make love without uttering loud cries of ecstasy. When it came to a serious talk about sensitive subjects, playing the radio and whispering wasn't going to do the job. I might feel compelled to yell out a few basic truths.

No, that talk we needed to have wasn't going to just happen. It would have to be a date.

I picked up the phone and called the boat shop. I got Joe's answering machine. I left a message. "Please call me, Joe." I called the house. I got our answering machine. I left a message. "Please call me immediately, Joe." I called Joe's cell phone. I got his voice mail. I left a message. "Call me the second you hear this, Joe, on pain of death."

But it was eight thirty, the workroom had been closed for hours, and Brenda and Tracy were cleaning the shop before Joe called back.

"What's up?"

How could he sound so casual? If I'd been mad at midafternoon, I was now steaming. Only the fact that Tracy and Brenda were standing fifteen feet away kept me from lacing into him with both sides of my tongue.

"Several things have come up today that need discussion," I said. "Can you come down here?"

"The shower's free at the moment, and I was thinking of getting into it. Can't we talk at home?"

"No."

Joe didn't respond for a moment. I was trying to keep my cool because of Brenda and Tracy, and he probably had Pete and Gina standing around behind him with their ears hanging out.

"I'll be there at nine," Joe said.

Joe got to the shop at eight fifty-five p.m., entering

by the front door. He helped finish up, sweeping the front of the shop while Tracy and Brenda cleaned and restocked the glass cases. I balanced the cash register. All the time Joe kept up a steady stream of Michigan State jokes—in Texas we call them Aggie jokes—while Tracy countered with some University of Michigan jokes, the same ones called Teasipper jokes in the Southwest. The girls enjoyed his performance.

I was still too mad to be amused, and Joe kept shooting significant glances in my direction all the time, so I gathered that he was nervous about what I was going to say. Somehow this made me madder than ever. Did he regard me as a witch with a capital B, a nagging wife who had to be placated? I determined to keep our discussion calm and rational.

After Joe walked Tracy and Brenda out to Brenda's car, which was parked in the alley, I met him in the break room, carrying the legal pad I'd used for my list of discussion topics.

"Uh-oh. This is serious stuff." Joe tapped the legal pad. "You had to make notes." Then Joe put his arms around me and nuzzled my neck. "Are we about to have our first fight? I'm already looking forward to making up."

I didn't push him away, but I wasn't very responsive either. *Rational,* I reminded myself. *Pretend this is a business conference.*

"One crazy thing after another happened today," I said. "Yes, I finally had to make a list."

Joe sat down on the comfortable couch Aunt Nettie had installed in the break room. I think he expected me to sit beside him, but instead I pulled a straight chair over and faced him.

"Shoot," he said.

"Well, since you mention shooting—were you aware that your pal Pete Falconer packs a pistol?"

Joe's face remained expressionless, so I went on. "I walked up on the porch when Pete wasn't expecting me, and he was stowing a large pistol in his duffel bag. What gives?"

Joe grinned. "I'm sure he has a permit," he said.

"A permit? Joe, Pete may have a dozen permits from the State of Michigan or the federal government or whoever else licenses firemen—I mean, firearms!"

I'd blown it. Joe knew I made those malapropisms when I was nervous. So much for my calm-and-rational act. I went on quickly. "But Pete does not have a permit to carry a pistol in my house! Our house."

"I didn't know you objected to firearms, Lee. I can even remember one occasion when you grabbed a deer rifle and threatened three people with it. You saved the day. You're a regular pistol-packin' mama when you're riled up."

I tried to keep my voice level. "Yes, I was raised with guns in the house, and I'm not afraid of them—if they're in the hands of people who practice handling them regularly and safely. But why does Pete need a pistol to watch birds?"

"Hey! Pete is well qualified in the handling of firearms. Just don't worry about it." Joe grinned again, but the grin didn't look natural.

"Do you know what Pete's up to?"

"I have some idea. And it is okay. Trust me on this one." Joe grinned even wider. "What's next on your list?"

I looked at it. "Gina."

"What about her?"

"Why is she here?"

"She's dodging her latest ex."

"Is he dangerous? Because if he is, Gina needs to be in a shelter, not in a house with two teenage girls."

"I don't think he's dangerous in the sense that he'll come looking for her. He may be dangerous in the sense that she's afraid he'll talk her into calling off the divorce."

"Who is he?"

"His name is Art Atkins."

"Atkins? Like your grandmother's maiden name?"

Joe laughed. "Yeah. Gina met him at a family reunion."

"Joe! Will you be serious?"

He patted my hand. "I'll try. Gina got acquainted with him through her antique business, though I think he actually is some sort of distant cousin."

"She's driving me crazy."

"I know Gina is annoying. Do you want me to throw her out?"

"Not if she really needs a place to stay. But will you try to convince her she should call your grandmother?" I described the episode when I'd been forced to lie to Joe's grandmother, to tell her—or at least imply—that I didn't know where Gina was, even though her missing daughter was running up my stairs.

Joe rolled his eyes. "I'll talk to Gina. What's next?"

He still didn't seem to be taking my concerns seriously, but I was down to one I thought would get his attention.

"Tracy overhead something at the grocery store that I found upsetting." I repeated the gossip linking Joe's mom to the burglaries along the lakeshore. "I made the girls promise they wouldn't repeat that story to anyone," I said.

I was surprised when Joe's first reaction was a shrug. "It's not like you to pay attention to gossip," he said.

"Joe! This isn't just gossip! This is slander! And it's completely unfair. Mercy should snow. I mean, sue! She should take that woman to court."

"Yeah, that would do a lot of good. That way the *Gazette* would write it up, and everybody in town would be talking about it. Like having a movie banned so you can sell more tickets."

"But what can we do about it?"

"We can't do anything about it. Except laugh it off. Yuk, yuk."

"That's all you've done with everything I've mentioned."

"Look, Lee, I know it's a mess having all these people at the house."

"And a big hole outside the back door."

"And a big hole outside the back door. I promise that Darrell and I will get some work done on that tomorrow. We'll try to have the whole project done in two weeks. All this is temporary. Pete will find his birds and leave. Gina will go home. Tracy's parents will get back, and she will go home. Summer will end, and Brenda will go back to Texas.

"See? Problems solved." He stood up. "I thought you hauled me down here to let me have it over the last item on your list."

He leaned over and tapped my legal pad, right on top of *Dinner with Garretts.*

"Actually, Joe, having you accept dinner engagements without consulting me is the least of my concerns. I haven't even mentioned the main problem yet."

"What's that?"

"Your dad came by the house this morning."

Joe's face went rigid. I'd finally gotten to something he didn't laugh off.

Chapter 6

Joe's expression became a glare. "That's not funny," he said.

"It didn't amuse me either, Joe. In fact, I almost slammed the door in the guy's face."

I described my encounter with the tall stranger with gray hair and a scarred cheek. "I thought you might know who he was," I said, "or what his visit was all about."

Joe was beginning to look more puzzled than angry. "I have no idea who he was or why he came."

"A high school coach? A law professor? There's never been anybody you thought of as a father? Anybody who thought of you as a son?"

"Not that I can think of. All the fathering I had—and I was lucky there—came from my mom's dad, Grandpa Matt."

"The boatbuilder?"

"Right. I used to hang out at his shop every afternoon. He taught me everything I know."

"About boats?"

"About life. I said I was lucky. This guy who came to the door—did you say he had a scar?"

"Yes. It wasn't disfiguring. In fact, he was quite an attractive man. The spooky thing was . . ." I stopped.

"He was wearing a sheet." Joe had lightened up a little.

"He wasn't *that* spooky! No, the thing that made my blood run cold was that his smile was reminiscent of yours."

"Mine?"

"Yes. I can't say he looked like you, except that he was tall and slim. And his hair had probably been dark when he was younger. But when he smiled . . . well, his face did take on a certain similarity to yours. Then, when I talked to Gina—"

"You told Gina about this?"

"I haven't told anybody. But I asked Gina about your dad—you know, what happened to him. I admit my stomach turned over when she said his ship went down in Lake Superior. I thought his grave might be empty, just a memorial. But she said that he was identified."

"Yeah. Mom had to identify him. Grandpa Matt went with her. She's never talked about it much. She did tell me she dreaded seeing him, but he didn't look bad." Joe sat down on the couch again. "That's one thing about Lake Superior. It's cold."

Yes, a drowning victim in Lake Superior is almost refrigerated. Superior is the farthest north of the Great Lakes, so it's largely fed by snowmelt. It also has the reputation of being the most dangerous lake, the most storm-tossed. They say that's because it's longest from east to west, so the prevailing winds have plenty of space to whip up high waves as a storm moves across it. Lake Superior's victims are often not found.

I shuddered and moved to the couch, sitting close to Joe.

"You never talk about your dad, Joe. I always assumed that you didn't remember him, since you were so small when he was killed."

"I was five. But he worked the Great Lakes freighters, so he was gone a lot even before he died. I don't think I understood what had happened—I remember that for a long time I'd ask Mom when he was coming home. Then she'd cry. I didn't understand why." He smiled ruefully. "She used to be happy when he came home."

I took his hand. "It must have been awfully hard for a little guy."

"Like I said, my grandfather fooled with me a lot. He explained that my dad wasn't coming home and why, but he had to do it several times before I caught on." Joe squeezed my hand. "But I assure you, Lee, that my father was actually, definitely dead. I remember the funeral a little."

"Gina says it was open-casket."

"I guess so. Mom must have whisked me out before the rest of the family. Anyway, I remember standing around outside afterward, waiting for my grandmother and Aunt Gina and a lot of other people to come out." He stared into space a moment, then gestured with the hand that held mine. "Okay. We know who didn't come to the door this morning. Now we've got to figure out who did. Was he driving?"

"Yes. A blue pickup. A Ford."

"Then it definitely wasn't my dad. The Atkins-Woodyard relatives are strictly GM."

We both chuckled. The American penchant to give the brand of the family cars and trucks the same weight as the family religion has always amused both Joe and me. True to his heritage, Joe drove a Chevy pickup.

"I don't suppose you got the license tag?" Joe said.

"I was so bumfuzzled I nearly didn't ask him for the phone number he refused to leave. But I'm sure it was a Michigan tag."

"A Michigan tag." Joe stared at the ceiling and slid his arm around me. I snuggled close to him, and we sat silently for at least sixty seconds.

"You know," I said, "you might have a good idea with that plan to have our first quarrel so we could make up."

"Hmm."

"This is the first time we've been alone in a week."

"Hmm."

"And Aunt Nettie did provide her break room with an awfully comfortable couch."

I snuggled even closer and gently nibbled Joe's ear.

"Scar!" He spoke so suddenly that I jumped. Then he whirled toward me. "Did you say the guy had a scar?"

"Yes, Joe. It ran down the side of his face. An old scar. It made him look kind of rakish."

"Ha!" Joe jumped to his feet. "Let me out the front door, okay?"

"Sure, but—"

"I thought of something I've got to check out."

So much for romance.

I didn't argue. Joe had been oblivious to my charms—not the usual state of affairs. He obviously had been struck by an idea. And when Joe gets an idea, I get out of his way.

So I let him out the front, then let myself out the back, feeling slightly miffed because he'd walked Brenda and Tracy to their car, but forgot to be chivalrous when it was my turn to leave. I didn't want him to turn into a male chauvinist pig like Pete, but still.

As I drove out onto Peach Street, I felt hungry, and that reminded me that I was going out to dinner the next day, but my houseguests would have to be fed. Luckily, the Superette had begun summer hours that week, so it would be open until eleven. That was enough time to get stew meat, carrots, and tomato soup for a simple Crock-Pot meal. Surely Gina could manage instant potatoes to go under it and ice cream for dessert. I got those items, plus two cartons of coleslaw from the deli. If ice cream wasn't enough for dessert, I'd snagged a few more chocolates from the discard tray. They'd gotten too hot and developed bloom, but the double fudge insides ("layers of milk and dark chocolate fudge in a dark chocolate coating") ought to satisfy anybody's sweet tooth.

I had to park at the Baileys' house and walk through the woods carrying my big brown bag of groceries and a small plastic bag holding Gina's paperback books, but I had a hand left for my flashlight. I found the living room empty. In fact, the whole house seemed empty. Joe's truck and Pete's SUV were there, but there was no sign of either of them. I could see a light in Darrell's camper, though, and when I checked upstairs Gina was lying on her bed, reading. I handed over her library books. Brenda and Tracy hadn't come home, she said.

I went down to the kitchen, poured myself a Diet Coke, and started assembling the stew. What I really wanted was a long, cool shower and a back rub from my bridegroom. A Diet Coke wasn't a good substitute.

I had the stew together and was rearranging the refrigerator so that I could cram the Crock-Pot into it when Joe and Pete came in the back door.

"Where have y'all been?" I said

"We've just been over at Darrell's," Joe said. "We're going to have a beer."

Joe got two bottles from the refrigerator, and he and Pete sat at the dining table. They were looking at

Pete's digital camera, but when I came through the room, Pete laid it on the table with the screen down. They didn't invite me to sit with them. It was definitely a stag conference.

I was too tired to try to horn my way into the conversation. I said good night to Pete, then took a shower. It was still so hot and so humid that I felt soggy when I got out. It was almost impossible to dry off.

Then I got into bed. I was so tired that I don't even remember Joe coming in, which might be considered a disgraceful way for a bride of three months to behave. He swears he kissed me good night, but I suspect he was as tired as I was and was careful not to disturb me. The next thing I knew it was six thirty a.m. It was still dark in the bedroom, even though we were a week past the summer solstice.

I love Michigan, but it has trees. In the case of Aunt Nettie's house—our house—there are a lot of trees, ranging from ten feet to a hundred feet tall, on the east side of the lot. The downstairs bedroom is on the west side of the house. This means we get up in the dark year-round, and in the summer even the dining room—on the east side of the house and with lots of windows—doesn't see any sun until midmorning. This is hard for a gal from the Texas plains to get used to.

But when the alarm went off, I got up, put on a pot of coffee, and got out the toast and cereal supplies. I left them on the dining table and got dressed in a chocolate brown TenHuis polo shirt and khaki slacks. Then I wrote a note about the dinner for Gina and headed for the office, leaving the do-it-yourself meal behind me. For once, the day at TenHuis Chocolade was routine. The counter help showed up, no unexpected emergency orders came in, and the tourists were no more obnoxious than usual. The air-conditioning limped along. With one unit doing the work of two, it wasn't exactly cool in the kitchens. Dolly watched the temperature in the storerooms carefully, and she had more boxes moved into the front of the shop. But the AC didn't break down completely.

I talked to Mrs. Vandemann, but all she could do was assure me that she was calling all over the state looking for a compressor for our system.

At five p.m., I left. When I arrived home—miracle of miracles—Gina had plugged in the Crock-Pot at the right time and seemed to grasp the concept of instant mashed potatoes and deli coleslaw. She called me "hon" only twice.

Darrell and Joe were working outside the bathroom, building forms for the foundation, but when they saw I was home, Joe declared the workday over. Joe got into the shower. Since I'd had the benefit of air-conditioning—my office was the coolest place at Ten-Huis Chocolade—I just changed into cream slacks and a shirt printed with green leaves on a cream background. I hoped it looked cool. Joe and I were ready to walk over to the Garretts' house at six thirty.

As we crossed Lake Shore Drive, I was glad to see that the Garretts had begun to make efforts at clearing out some of the brush that had made the Double Diamond cottage look spooky. It was a lovely old place. Garnet came to meet us as we walked up the steps.

"What's happened to the cool Michigan summer?" she said.

"It'll be back," Joe said. "But maybe you won't want to serve drinks on the porch tonight."

"All we have in the way of air-conditioning is a window unit," she said. "Central air is in our plan of action for after our ship comes in. Do you like gin and tonic? It always cools me off."

I gave her the chocolates, and she introduced me to Dick Garrett. A balding fellow with a broad grin, he was much taller than his tiny wife. He and Garnet gave us an abbreviated tour of the inside of the house—the living room and dining room overlooked the lake, of course. The tour ended with a walk down a flagstone path leading to a deck perched on the top of the bluff overlooking the beach. These decks are common along our section of Lake Michigan, where banks from eight to twenty feet tall loom above the shore. Wooden steps led down to Double Diamond's private stretch of sand and pebbles.

Back in the house Dick and Joe moved to a bar set up on a table in the corner of the living room and began to talk boats while Dick measured gin and squeezed limes into tall glasses.

Shade trees and the window unit made the living room temperature bearable. Garnet motioned me to a couch that sat at a right angle to a brick fireplace. The fireplace stood out because of its beauty; the rest of the decor had a shabby feel. The couch was sprung, and the flowers in its upholstery were faded. The hardwood floor was scuffed and scarred. A graceful Craftsman-style library table stood against the back wall, but the rest of the furniture was like ours—used, not antique. The room had dark walls that seemed to soak up the light from the two or three small lamps. The windows overlooked the lake, true, but trees and the broad-roofed porch would keep sunlight out for another hour.

I guess the dim atmosphere was what kept me from seeing the other guest. I jumped when a voice suddenly spoke out of the gloom.

"Are you and your husband related to Gina Woodyard?"

A tiny little man was sitting in a wicker rocker at

the end of the couch. I can't call him gnomelike, because that implies baldness. This man was small and wizened, but he was not bald. Thick, wavy white hair was combed back from his face and crawled down over his collar.

Before I could answer, Garnet spoke. "This is my uncle Alex. Alex Gold."

I put on my gracious-guest face. "Of course. You mentioned that your uncle would be here." Alex Gold was too far away to shake hands with, so I nodded, and he lifted a glass filled with clear liquid in reply. I saw ice cubes and an olive in the bottom and decided it was a martini on the rocks. No G and T for Uncle Alex.

"Gina Woodyard is Joe's aunt," I said. I didn't tell Alex that Gina was within a few hundred feet of him, hiding out. "How do you know her?"

"Everyone in the Midwest antique world knows Gina."

"I knew she had an antique shop."

He waved his martini. "Her shop isn't all that important. It's her expertise."

I must have looked as blank as I felt, because he spoke again. "Surely you know she's one of the nation's top experts on costume jewelry."

"Actually, I didn't know. But I've been in the Woodyard family for only three months."

"I see that your husband gave you a beautiful stone for your wedding ring."

I held up my ring: a broad gold band with a single not-too-large diamond mounted in a Tiffany setting. "The diamond came from Joe's grandmother's engagement ring. His grandparents married in the mid-thirties."

Alex Gold slithered out of his seat, kneeling beside me. He took my hand with a clammy paw. I wanted to pull away, but he shoved my hand under the dim light at the end of the couch.

"The stone is older than the mid-thirties," he said. "That antique cut was popular before 1920."

"Joe!" I wanted to get away from Gold so badly that I almost squawked. "Mr. Gold says your grandmother's diamond is older than the mid-thirties!"

Joe stopped talking and looked around absentmindedly. "Actually, Grandma inherited the diamond from her mother," he said. "My grandfather didn't have a lot of money in 1935, so they had this diamond she already owned reset as an engagement ring. My grandmother always wore it when I was a kid. I wanted Lee to have it, so we had it reset again."

Mr. Gold scooted back into his wicker rocker. He nodded complacently. "I don't have a loupe, but it looks like a Tolkowsky cut. You should write down its provenance. These stories are so easily lost."

My gin and tonic arrived then, so I was able to quiz Alex Gold about his connection with the antique trade.

"I own a jewelry shop in Chicago," he said. "Gold chains and engagement rings pay the rent. But I have an interest in antique jewelry."

Garnet spoke. "Uncle Alex is one of the world's leading experts on Art Deco jewelry."

Alex looked modest. "I'm to Art Deco jewelry what your aunt is to costume jewelry. I've researched it extensively, and I do appraisals."

"Then you've kept up your grandmother's interest in precious stones."

"Our grandmother was somewhat interested in their beauty, true, but to her their importance lay mainly in their value." He smiled. "Her admirers were expected to cough up major stones. I'm more interested in design and workmanship. Your diamond wouldn't have impressed Grandmother Opal, because it's not particularly large—half a carat, I'd say—but I like it better than a larger stone that might not have such a lovely cut."

Garnet interceded then, like a good hostess, asking me about our wedding and making other attempts at small talk. Her uncle sat with us, ignoring the boat discussion between Joe and Dick Garrett. In a few minutes, however, Garnet called Joe and Dick over and the conversation became general. Alex didn't grab my hand again, and his open admiration of my diamond—I also thought it was lovely—had made him seem less creepy.

After an hour of chitchat, Dick braved the heat to go outside and charcoal steaks. Garnet brought baked potatoes and salad from the kitchen, and we moved to the dining table. The sun had gone down by the time we finished off with locally grown strawberries topped with sugar and cream, and Garnet passed the TenHuis chocolates as she served coffee. I had a Dutch Caramel Bonbon ("creamy, European-style soft caramel wrapped in dark chocolate"). By the time we'd all accepted a final cup of coffee it was dark. The evening had turned out to be very pleasant.

Like many of the summer cottages along Lake Michigan, Double Diamond had no shades or curtains on its windows. The dining room's wall was made up entirely of windows—double-hung windows, with wainscoting below. A set of French doors was at one end. Beyond the windows was a section of the cottage's broad porch and, beyond that, trees and the lake. After dark, the porch, trees, and lake disappeared, as if the lights on a stage had been turned off, and the wall of windows became a wall of mirrors. I happened to be seated facing the windows.

So I was the one who saw the face.

At first the face was just a blob, sort of like a balloon tied to a chair outside the window. It moved, and I thought I was seeing a reflection of one of the people inside the house.

I counted heads. There was Dick Garrett at the end of the table. I wasn't seeing his reflection. He'd be in profile, not facing the window. Besides, Dick was telling some story and was gesturing wildly, and I could see him in the window clearly. No, it wasn't Dick.

It wasn't Joe. Joe was facing me, so his back was to the windows. It wasn't Garnet. The face outside was topped by what appeared to be dark hair, not strawberry blond.

That meant it had to be Alex. But no, Alex had white hair. He was sipping his coffee and giving his full attention to his niece's husband. I located his reflection in the wall of windows. It wasn't the one I could see.

The face belonged to a stranger.

I turned to Garnet and spoke in a low voice, trying not to interrupt Dick's yarn. "Excuse me, but there seems to be someone on the porch."

Garnet turned her head toward the windows.

Joe didn't bother to be polite. He spoke up loudly. "What's wrong?"

Garnet's eyebrows raised. "Lee says there's someone on the porch."

Joe was halfway out of his chair when the door to the deck swung open, and the man came into the room. At that moment I couldn't have told you what he looked like.

All I could see was the shiny silver pistol in his hand.

Chapter 7

"**E**verybody stay still," the man said. "We don't want any trouble."

I think we were all too astonished to give him any, especially after a second man with a second pistol came through the front door and ran across the living room to join our little tableau. With frightening calm, the two ordered us to keep our seats. When Joe remained hunched over, half standing and apparently undecided about whether or not he was going to drop his fanny onto his chair, the first man pointed his pistol at me. I'm happy to report that Joe quickly sat down.

Neither he nor Dick Garrett looked happy, but they didn't start a fight.

"Nobody's going to get hurt," the first man said. "We'll have to make sure you don't follow us, but you'll get loose without much trouble."

The second man produced a roll of duct tape. As I mentally reviewed the numerous cases in which people were bound and gagged, then murdered, he looped it around each of us, securing us to our chair backs, but he didn't wrap our feet—or even our hands. Just our upper arms. And he didn't gag us.

By then my brain was beginning to function, and I tried to notice what the two guys looked like. One was tall and slim and the other short and not so slim. The difference in their heights was striking. And that was all I could tell.

Their mothers couldn't have recognized them, except that they seemed to be sports fanatics. They wore wet suits over their bodies and ski masks over their heads. Both wore latex gloves. Their getups were effective—I couldn't tell a thing about either of them.

I even looked at their feet. They wore rubber clogs of a type available in every drugstore, discount store, and department store in the United States. I couldn't even see whether either of them had a bunion or an ingrown toenail.

Dick Garrett muttered his opinion of their family heritage as the duct tape went around his shoulders, but Garnet spoke to him sharply. "Keep quiet!" she said. "Please!"

Dick obeyed, and both armed men seemed to ignore his comments.

The only one of us who acted brave—or maybe nonchalant—was Alex Gold. "I always expected to be held up at the store," he said. "Not here, where there's nothing to steal." He folded his hands as if praying, holding them over his plate as the tape went around his shoulders.

After all five of us were well taped, the two invaders simply stood there. I found myself wondering if they didn't know what to do next. Shouldn't they be demanding that we empty our pockets and take off our jewelry? I wiggled my hand, twisting my wedding ring around to hide its stone.

But still the two men did nothing but stand there watching us. Finally the tall one spoke. "Go yell at him," he said.

Yell at him?

The shorter, rounder masked man left the dining room, and seconds later I heard him yell, "Hurry!"

And a strange voice echoed into the room, apparently from upstairs. "What's happened?"

"Blondie spotted us. Everything's under control. But hurry! Don't worry about being quiet!"

The short guy came back into the dining room. He and the taller man stood at either end of the dining table, staring at us—their captives—but again neither said a word. They were obviously waiting for the guy upstairs.

Then I heard light steps on the stairs. The guy up there was obviously not wearing heavy rubber clogs.

"Got it!" The third man came into the dining room. He was tall and thin, and he wore the same wet suit–ski mask outfit the others had on, but he had different shoes. They looked like black oxfords, but they weren't. This guy did have a bunion, and I could see where it warped the shape of his right shoe. I wouldn't have been able to see that if he'd been wearing leather oxfords.

This third man stopped and surveyed the room, and I saw that he was carrying a blue denim bag. "Let's go," he said.

That was when Uncle Alex lost it. "No! No!" he screamed like a teakettle. He jumped in his chair. His face was contorted. With fury? With fear? What?

We all stared at him. He gave a final shriek, twitched madly, and went over backward. His feet caught the edge of the table, and it leaped in the air, rattling the dishes. Garnet yelled, "Uncle Alex! Uncle Alex!" and Dick began to swear again.

The back legs of Alex's chair slid on the rug, and he fell, landing flat on his back on the hardwood floor, chair and all. He lay there gasping.

I don't know what I did or said, but when I looked at Joe, he was standing up—as well as he could stand up with a chair taped to his back. To my amazement, I saw a knife in his hand.

"Turn around!" He yelled the words at Dick.

Dick obeyed him, scooting his chair sideways. I saw that Joe had a steak knife like the ones we'd used at dinner. It must have been left on the table when Garnet cleared the dishes. Joe had apparently palmed it while he was hovering over his chair earlier. Joe slit the tape along Dick's back, parallel to the back of his chair.

And I realized that the three men in wet suits were gone. They must have run out while Alex was having his fit. The door to the deck was standing open, and I could hear the rubber clogs thumping. The sound was getting fainter.

Garnet wasn't yelling now, but she kept talking. "Uncle Alex? Uncle Alex, are you all right?"

Dick came out of his chair then, twisting to get the tape off, and he took the knife and sawed at the duct tape that held Joe. He then freed Garnet and after her, me.

By the time Dick got to me, Joe had stripped off the tape and was running toward the front door, on the opposite side of the house from where the men had run out.

"Joe! Joe! Stop!" He didn't seem to hear me, but he did pause long enough to turn the porch light off before he opened the door. Then he disappeared into the dark.

I peeled the duct tape off my shirt and jumped out of my chair. Garnet and Dick were kneeling beside

Alex, freeing him from his duct tape. He was breathing regularly. They didn't need me.

So I ran out the front door after Joe.

Out on the porch, of course, I had to stop immediately. Coming from light to dark, even the dim light of the living and dining rooms, I couldn't see a thing. I plastered my back to the wall beside the door and listened. I could hear someone moving to my right. He stumbled as he went off the porch. I assumed it was Joe.

The front door of the house faced south, and as I'd seen when we walked over, the trees on that side had been cleared out a bit. But it was pitch-dark as I edged my way along the porch. I thought of going back inside, but I was too worried about Joe.

I'd figured out that he'd run out the front, instead of following the robbers through the door that faced the lake, because he didn't want to be silhouetted against the dining room windows. But the three crooks might be lying in ambush for any pursuers. . . .

I kept edging along the porch, keeping my back to the wall, working toward the side of the house that faced the lake. As I got near the corner, the kitchen and dining room windows were lighting up the back of the house, and I began to be able to see more. I stopped at the steps that led to the flagstone path, the one we had followed out to the deck overlooking the lake. I stood there, trying to look beyond the pool of light from the living and dining rooms and to see what was happening out there in the darkness.

And I heard a motorboat.

It roared suddenly. It was obviously right offshore, out in Lake Michigan, near the Double Diamond beach.

"They're escaping by boat." It still seemed that I ought to be quiet, so I whispered the words.

I began to go down the flagstone walk as quickly as possible. I didn't run. There was no moon, and once I was away from the house the area was still as dark as the darkest chocolate in Aunt Nettie's shop. But I managed to make my way to the deck that overlooked the lake.

A man was standing on that deck, and I recognized the shape of him. It was Joe.

"Did they get away?" I said.

"I guess so. I didn't follow closely enough to see all the details. I wasn't eager to get shot."

I threw my arms around him. "You scared me to death, running out like that!"

Joe patted me on the back. "I'm not dumb enough to get killed over somebody else's jewelry."

"Jewelry? Is that what they took?"

"It's gotta be. Alex is a jeweler, and he was calm as a millpond until he saw that denim bag. Then he got hysterical."

The sound of the boat was fading. I heard footsteps behind us, and the beam of a flashlight came bouncing down the walk toward us.

"Joe! Lee!" Dick was coming.

Joe answered him. "We're here, Dick! They got away."

Dick came up to us, panting. He barely paused, then started down the steps toward the beach. But Joe caught his arm.

"Dick, I think they went off in that boat. We'd better stay away from the beach until the cops get here. By some fluke they might have left a clue. A footprint or a beach shoe. Something."

Dick stopped and growled.

I spoke quickly. "How's Alex?"

"The old bastard's fine. If he would have used a

courier service like he should have . . ." Dick turned to Joe. "They've ripped out the phone line, and my cell phone won't work out here on the lakeshore."

Cell phone service is quirky along the lake. Some companies have good service, and some don't.

"I'll run to our house and call the cops," Joe said. "You stay here."

I remembered that I ought to be a helpful guest, so I went back into the house with Dick. Alex was free, and his chair had been placed upright. He was sitting in it, holding his head in his hands. And moaning.

"Oh, oh, oh. Oh, Garnet, I've wrecked your inheritance. Oh, oh, oh."

"Oh, Uncle Alex, do be quiet," Garnet said sharply. "You didn't do it on purpose. You're not hurt seriously, and none of the rest of us is hurt at all. That's what's important."

Alex wasn't comforted. As a matter of fact, Garnet didn't look very comforted either, and Dick prowled up and down the room silently. We sat at the ravaged dinner table until Joe came back and said the Warner Pier police were on their way.

Dick snorted. "The WPPD. Big deal!"

"I recommended that the acting chief call in the state police," Joe said.

Dick shorted again. "How likely are they to do what you ask?"

"Pretty likely," Joe said.

His voice was cold. I could tell he was losing his patience with Dick Garrett, so I spoke up. "Joe is Warner Pier City Attorney, and my aunt is married to the police chief." They might as well know the worst about their neighbors. "I think the acting chief will listen to Joe."

"One of the functions of the Michigan State Police

is to help small municipalities with investigations," Joe said. "They'd be called in for any major robbery."

We heard the sirens then. "At least they're fast," Dick said.

Alex was still moaning, and Garnet was still glaring at him.

Then the siren was too loud for us to talk any more, so I sat down again and waited, ready to cooperate with the authorities.

And wait was about all I did for the next couple of hours.

The state police were there fairly quickly, but it took longer for the crime scene lab to arrive, since it's stationed in Grand Rapids, sixty miles away. We each gave a preliminary statement, but the wet suits and ski masks had been effective. I was the only one who had seen anything else, and a bunion isn't really an uncommon feature of a man's foot. And, as anybody familiar with the beaches would expect, no useful tracks were likely to be found there. Running or walking across a Lake Michigan beach just leaves indefinite holes where each foot was placed. Only wet sand would show real tracks.

The men had apparently not dropped anything as they ran across the beach. No ski masks, rubber clogs, matchbooks, sunglasses, or driver's licenses were found.

The most interesting thing was hearing Alex's explanation for having valuable jewelry hidden in his denim laundry bag. And it was valuable. I didn't get to read the list he produced, but the state police investigator blinked several times and gave a low whistle.

"I've carried millions of dollars worth of jewelry in my pockets all over the country," Alex said defensively. "Lots of jewelers do that. I've never had any problem."

"But you weren't carrying just any jewelry this time." Dick's voice was gruff. "It was the Diamonte collection."

"I know! And I can't imagine why anyone would want to steal it."

"Why not?" the state policeman asked.

"It's too well-known. Many of these pieces have been displayed in museums. And all of it is documented—photos of the jewelry have appeared in reference books. Selling it would be like trying to pawn the Mona Lisa."

The state cop looked up from the list. "Then they'll have to break it up."

Alex appeared to shrink. "God! I hope not. That would be a tragedy!"

"Why did you have it with you, anyway?"

"It's a family farewell visit! Dick and Garnet's children are coming next week. Each family member was to select a piece to keep as a memento. Then I was to take it to Christie's in New York for sale."

"It was to be auctioned off?"

Alex nodded numbly. "My niece and I had decided it should be sold. No one wore the jewelry, no one really enjoyed it. We had to keep it locked in the vault in my store. And even that had to be a secret. Garnet and Dick's son is entering medical school. The collection would eventually benefit him and his sister. It seemed more sensible to sell it now, so that young Rick wouldn't have to face the debt all those additional years of education might require."

Alex moaned again. "And now I've ruined that plan!"

Garnet put her arm around her uncle. "Uncle Alex, please don't be so upset. First, the collection belongs to you. If I get a share of the sale, it's simply out of the goodness of your heart. Second, you told me that the collection was insured and that the insurance included the period of transportation."

"Yes, it was insured, Garnet. But not for enough. I hoped to get twice the amount of the insurance at the sale. The insurance will barely cover the loan."

"Loan? What loan?"

Now I could see that Alex had tears in his eyes. "Garnet, two years ago—when business got so bad— I needed money to keep the shop going."

"Oh, Uncle Alex!"

"Yes, Garnet. I used the collection as collateral for a loan. Even if the insurance pays off fully, I'll have barely enough to pay the bank."

Chapter 8

Alex's confession embarrassed me. I felt sorry for Garnet and Dick. They seemed to be nice people, and it was unpleasant to think that the robbery meant a serious financial loss to them, and possibly a family split over Alex's actions. But learning more than I needed to know about the Gold/Garrett family finances wasn't a large concern to me.

My concern was getting out of there. I wanted to go home, where I wouldn't have to keep up a brave face. It was beginning to be an effort to keep my upper lip stiff.

Finally the cops said Joe and I could go. Which led to the most terrifying part of the whole evening—walking home in the dark.

In our neighborhood, there are streetlights only at widely spaced intervals, and there are lots of trees in between. Some of the houses have outdoor lights, of course, but in summer the thick foliage keeps the ground dark, especially when there's no moon. And there was no moon that night.

We had brought along a nice big flashlight, knowing

that we'd probably be walking home after sunset. So we set out confidently. But I was clutching Joe's hand.

All was well as we went down the long drive that led away from the Double Diamond cottage. It wasn't lit, but the cop cars were still parked along the way. Between the lights the cops were using and the flashlight Joe was carrying, we could see pretty well. So I managed until we got to Lake Shore Drive.

That was when a dog barked about ten feet away from us.

I did an Olympic-style broad jump and landed on the other side of the road. The only thing that kept me from heading up our lane—breaking the hundred-yard dash record as I went—was that I was still holding Joe's hand tightly; I had to pull him along like a rowboat dragging an anchor. Although Joe claims he jumped even farther than I did at the first bark.

Then I recognized the yapping. "Alice, you darling little dog, you startled me," I said. Well, those may not have been the exact words I used.

"Hush up, Alice!" The voice coming out of the dark belonged to Harold Glick, of course. "Joe? Lee?"

Joe spoke. "Harold? What are you doing?"

"Trying to figure out what all the cop cars are doing here. What's happened?"

"The Lake Shore crime wave hit the Garretts," Joe said. "Lee and I were innocent bystanders."

Harold, of course, wanted to know all the details. Why shouldn't he, since he didn't have anything else to interest him? Besides, he was proud of his status as the burglars' first victim.

Joe declined to tell him anything. "Lee's frazzled," he said. "So am I. We're going home."

"But did they catch the guys?"

By now we were far enough away that Joe called back over his shoulder, "Tomorrow, Harold."

Alice barked good-bye.

The encounter with Harold and Alice was the end of the line for me. During the time we'd been held at gunpoint, I'd been afraid to move. Then the robbers had run off, and Joe had followed them. That was when I'd really gotten scared. I'd followed Joe outside not out of bravery, but out of terror. My adrenaline had been in overdrive. I'd been energized, ready to "fight or flee," as they say. But an hour of sitting still waiting around to talk to the detectives had left me trembling. The adrenaline had waned, and the nerves had waxed. When a fierce beast like Alice loomed out of the darkness, my nerves gave up. I wanted to get home and collapse.

When we got to the house, Pete was waiting on the porch. He came across the yard to meet us. Ignoring Joe, he grabbed my hands. "Are you all right, girl?"

In the beam of Joe's flashlight, I could see he really looked concerned. It should have pleased me, I guess, but his attitude infuriated me instead.

"Ask Joe if *he's* all right," I said angrily. "He's the one who chased the robbers. I only sat in the living room like a perfect lady."

Then our other four houseguests ran out to greet us, all babbling questions. I pushed my way through the throng and walked into the house without a word. I went into the bedroom, closed the door, and lay down on the bed. I felt like crying, but Pete had made me so mad that I didn't.

The hubbub died after I closed the door. In a minute the door opened, and I heard Joe's footsteps. I just kept lying there.

When Joe spoke, his voice sounded scared. "You okay?"

"No!"

"Oh." He stood beside the bed, shifting his weight from foot to foot. Then he turned on the window fan that pulled damp air in from outside. I wouldn't look at him. But he kept standing there, so I finally had to.

Joe looked so forlorn I began to laugh. When he heard that laugh, he looked terrified.

"I'm not hysterical," I said. "I just had to let it soak in a few minutes."

"You were really brave back at the Garretts'," Joe said.

"That was an act," I said.

Then Joe got onto the bed beside me and put his arms around me, tight. We didn't even move. We just held each other and breathed. We were completely silent.

Sometimes Joe does know exactly the right thing to say.

After about five minutes, I sighed. "I'd better go assure everybody that I'm all right."

"You did scare them. Scared me, too."

"Back at the Garretts', you scared me. Picking up that steak knife! Running after those guys! I can't do without you, Joe! Please don't be brave anymore."

"You notice I wasn't brave enough to follow the robbers down onto the beach, where there wasn't anything to hide behind."

"Thank God!"

We gave each other a kiss, then got up. I combed my hair, and we went back out into the living room, where everybody was sitting around with big eyes. They looked at me as if I were a bomb about to explode.

"I'm fine now," I said. "I just had to collapse a minute."

Apparently Brenda, Tracy, Gina, Pete, and Darrell

had each been holding his or her breath, because a collective hiss sounded as each of them gave a gentle, "Whew." Then they all started talking again, but this time it didn't make me crazy.

Brenda—who's learning the most effective ways to handle stress—got a box of TenHuis chocolates from the refrigerator and passed them around. An Amaretto Truffle ("milk chocolate interior coated in white chocolate with milk chocolate stripes") made me feel much better.

Joe and I, both talking at once, gave a stirring account of the experience of being held at gunpoint. Pretty soon we found something to laugh about—I think it was the robbers standing around as if they didn't know what to do next—and our laughter had a hysterical edge, but that was all right.

By then it was past midnight. Gina yawned and headed toward the bathroom. After Gina went up to bed, Tracy and Brenda took their turns at toothbrushing and face-washing, and then went upstairs. Darrell went out to his camper.

Only Pete kept his seat. I wondered if he was waiting until Joe and I cleared out of the living room, since his porch opened off it, and he might want to go to bed with some privacy. So I patted Joe on the knee. "I guess I'll say good night, too."

But Pete leaned forward, looking serious. "Would you mind talking to me for a minute first?"

"Sure," I said. Was I actually going to have a conversation with Pete Falconer? Emboldened by the harrowing experiences I'd had that evening, I made a vow: If Joe wasn't going to tell me what Pete was up to, I'd ask him myself.

"Let me get my stuff," Pete said. He went out onto the porch, turned on the light, and dug through his belongings. Somehow I wasn't surprised when he came back with his camera.

Joe and I sat on the couch, and Pete pulled a wicker rocker over so that our six knees were nearly touching.

"This looks awfully official, Pete," I said, "coming from a bird-watcher."

Pete grinned his macho grin. "I wanted to show you a few snapshots." He kept his voice just above a whisper, and I thought of Gina, just six or eight feet above our heads. Over the past few days Pete had learned how easy it was to eavesdrop in our house.

Pete brought pictures up on his camera one at a time, and showed them to me. He'd called them snapshots, and that was what they were, at least technically. They were very ordinary pictures of two guys walking up and down the beach. Both of them wore standard Warner Pier garb—khaki shorts and T-shirts. One was tall and slim and wore a green shirt. The other was short and round and wore a navy or black shirt with lettering on the front.

The subjects didn't seem to be aware of the camera at all, and the photos had been taken from the bank above the beach, not from the beach itself.

I was sure the people in the pictures hadn't known they were being photographed.

"Pretty unusual birds you've been photographing, Pete," I said. "What did you do? Set up a deer stand in the bushes?"

Pete looked surprised, and Joe gave a guttural laugh. "I told you she was smart," he said.

"These were obviously taken repetitiously," I said. "I mean, surreptitiously! The people didn't know they were having their pictures taken. What's the deal?"

"First, do you recognize either of the men in the photos?"

I looked at them again. "That's our beach, of course. Beech Tree Public Access Area, right down the road. That tree—that's the one the kids from down the road tried to build a tree house in last year. As for the people, no, I don't recognize them."

"I wanted to make sure neither of these guys was the one who came to the door yesterday."

"Joe told you about that? No, I'm sure he isn't one of them. I can't see the face of the one in the dark shirt, but he looks too short. And the tall one's hair is too dark."

"Could they be the guys who invaded the Garretts' house?"

I looked at the pictures carefully. "They could be, Pete. All I could tell about the robbers was that the first one was taller and slimmer than the second one, and the second one was shorter and rounder than the first. And that would certainly describe these two. But I'm sure neither of the guys in these pictures is the man who came from upstairs."

I tapped the camera. "However, I certainly couldn't pick any of the three guys who were at the Garretts out of a lineup. Unless I saw the one guy's feet."

"Feet?"

"Yeah," Joe said. "Lee says the guy who rummaged around upstairs had a bunion."

"Big deal," I said. "The state police didn't seem impressed by that observation."

Pete frowned, and I spoke again. "Are those all your questions, Pete?"

"Yeah."

"Then you can answer a couple from me." I took a deep breath. "Who are you, and what are you doing here?"

Pete frowned, and Joe laughed. They looked at each

other; then Pete spoke. "I'm just an innocent bird-watcher, Lee. And I'm going to bed."

He stood up, said good-night, and left for the bathroom.

I was furious. I jumped to my feet and started after Pete. But Joe had jumped to his feet, too, and he grabbed me. "Wait a minute, Lee!"

"Joe! This is my house. I deserve to know what's going on!"

Joe didn't say a word. He kissed me.

I shoved him away, but it took me a minute. Joe's a great kisser. But I ducked out of his arms.

"Cut it out, Joe! I'm serious!" I stormed after Pete.

Joe's interference had allowed Pete enough time to get into the bathroom and lock the door before I could go through the kitchen and reach the back hall. I raised my hand to bang on the door, but stopped. I didn't want to cause a commotion that would bring Gina and the girls downstairs. Especially not Tracy. She was trying hard not to gossip, but a shouting match with Pete might be too tempting a tidbit to keep quiet. It might be all over town by ten tomorrow morning.

Besides, if Pete was determined not to tell me what was going on, I could bang on the door all night and he probably wouldn't change his mind.

I lowered my fist, spun around, and went into our bedroom by its back door. Joe followed me.

"Lee, you'll just have to trust Pete and me on this," he said.

"I'll be glad to trust you, Joe, but I don't know Pete well enough to trust him. How long have you known him?"

"Since I got out of law school. I've always found him very reliable."

"Is he another of your former clients?"

Joe laughed. "Actually, I guess he is. Lee . . ."

I held up my hand in a gesture I hoped said, *halt.* "I don't want to know," I said. Joe seemed determined to fill the house with people who'd once been accused of some crime or other, and I was not very happy about it.

Joe and I stared at each other for what seemed to be five minutes, but was actually about five seconds. Then Joe spoke. "I'll lock the house up."

"That'll do a lot of good," I said. "Lock all the doors, but leave the windows wide open so we won't smother. Lordy! I'm tired of this heat!"

Joe left me to snarl at the bedspread as I yanked it off the bed. I was in a foul temper, and I knew I should cool down. But how could I cool off emotionally when it was after midnight and it was so hot I was ready to simply burn up and the humidity was so high that I couldn't burn, I could only boil?

An evening with cool air from the pitiful little window unit at the Garretts' house had left me feeling terribly sorry for myself. Because of the casement windows my great-grandfather had installed in our house, there wasn't a single place where we could put an air conditioner without cutting a hole in a wall. Our fans only blew the humid air around. My skin was covered with a film of sweat.

I couldn't even take my clothes off, because the cops and Harold Glick—and probably a dozen other people—were roaming around the neighborhood, and we couldn't close our windows or pull our curtains because of the heat. The only place I could dress and undress after sundown was the bathroom, where we did have coverings for the windows, and Pete—darn him anyway!—was in there.

Once I had the bed down to the bottom sheet, I

did lie down on it with the window fan blowing right on me. By the time Joe came back in, I was calm enough to tell him I was sorry for yelling. "I'm not sorry for what I said," I told him, "but I'm sorry I said it in an ugly voice."

"I'm sorry Pete annoys you so much. I'm not sure I understand why. Frankly, most women like him."

"Maybe that's one thing I don't like about him— that air of being God's gift to the opposite sex." I rolled over and leaned on my elbow. "Let's be frank here. I think he reminds me of Rich."

I wasn't sure I should have told Joe that. Rich was my first husband.

Joe laughed. "I guess I should be happy to hear that," he said. He sat on the edge of the bed and pulled off his shoes. "This heat is wearing us all down. Surely it will break soon."

I rolled back over, then spoke. "Joe, do you think the robbery tonight is part of the lakeshore crime wave?"

"It breaks the pattern. All the other crimes were what you might call standard burglaries—second-degree burglary, a break-in when no one was threatened. The other houses were empty."

"And this was a home invasion," I said.

"Yes. Aggravated robbery, robbery when the robber is armed with a deadly weapon. A different crime legally."

"Not entirely different, Joe. As I reconstruct what happened, the upstairs guy broke in and was looking for the jewels while the other two kept watch. If he'd found the jewels before we saw the group outside, he would have left the same way he came in—by an upstairs window or however he got in. His pals would have crept away after him, and none of us would have been the wiser until Alex wanted to put his dirty underwear in his denim bag."

"You blew their plan, Lee, when you saw the guy on the porch."

"He shouldn't have gotten so close to the window."

"True. He goofed. Once he'd been spotted, they had to come in and tie us all up. But if you hadn't seen them, it would have been simply a burglary. So maybe it does fit the MO."

"But they definitely were after the Diamonte jewels. They didn't take my ring or make you and Dick empty your wallets."

That seemed to be all either of us had to say on the subject, and I heard Pete come out of the bathroom, so I went in. About the time I turned off my tepid shower it began to rain gently. Considering how hot and miserable the weather had been, that could have been a good thing. But instead of breaking the miserable humidity, the rain seemed simply to accentuate it. So in addition to having a nervous night— being held at gunpoint always disturbs my rest—Joe and I were also physically miserable, lying on damp sheets with a fan blowing wet air over us. If God had wanted people to live with high humidity, He wouldn't have invented central air.

I finally fell soundly asleep about four a.m. and didn't wake up until after eight. Luckily, Gina had made coffee for the gang. Double luckily, it was my day off. The skies were still gray, but the drizzle had stopped.

When I staggered to the table, barefoot and still in the T-shirt and shorts I'd slept in, Gina and Joe were sitting on either side of the toaster. Joe wore gym shorts and a T-shirt. Gina wore tight pink pants, a bright blue tunic, and pink high heels. On her shoulder was a pin featuring a poodle with a semiclear pink tummy, and pink plastic earrings hung from her ears.

I roused enough to ask about the rest of the

houseguests, and Gina said everyone else had eaten.
Joe said Pete had gone someplace to watch birds—
like I believed that—and Brenda and Tracy had left
for the shop. Darrell was in his camper. I could see
all his doors and windows were open, and his fan was
going so hard it must have been like a wind tunnel
in there.

I was drinking coffee and wondering if I had enough
energy to drop a piece of bread in the toaster, when
someone knocked at the back door. Gina rapidly tiptoed into the living room, and Joe went into the
kitchen.

The door was standing open, of course. I could hear
Alice scratch on the screen.

"Hi, Harold," Joe said.

"Joe! I've got a great idea about how to fight these
burglaries. We need to form a neighborhood watch."

I let my head sink into my hands. All I wanted to
do was go back to bed, and here was Harold, ready
to hold a meeting.

I'm happy to say that Joe didn't invite Harold in.
He stepped out onto the porch to talk to him. But I
could hear every word they said.

"A neighborhood watch?" Joe said. "I don't know
how that would work out here where the houses aren't
very close together."

"That's why we need one!" Alice gave a yap, apparently to encourage him.

Harold went on. "We could have patrols."

"A lot of the summer places have alarms," Joe said.

"I know. But they don't seem to be doing much
good."

"I don't know, Harold. It seems to me that the main
value of a neighborhood watch is to encourage people
to get to know their neighbors—you know, so they
know who's out of town and stuff like that. And out

here . . . well, we pretty much know one another
already."

"You and Lee do, maybe. I know most of the permanent residents. But the summer people—I don't
know them at all."

"You will before the end of the summer."

Harold took Joe's comment as a compliment. "I
try," he said modestly. "And Alice helps. Everybody
likes Alice."

I grinned. Yes, the lonely Harold with his cute mutt
would know everybody for miles around by the end
of the summer.

I barely caught Joe's sigh. "It's certainly an idea,
Harold. Why don't you talk to the city clerk on Monday? She'll tell you how to go about setting up a
neighborhood watch. But it won't be easy, because of
the summer people. They're not interested in going
to meetings."

"If we had lists of everybody's license tag numbers,"
Harold said, "if we knew who was supposed to be in
the neighborhood and who wasn't, then we might be
able to catch those guys in the act."

"The summer people have houseguests all the time,
Harold. That's one of the reasons people buy these
places. So it would be hard to keep track of license
numbers."

Harold nodded. "I know, I know. But they still hear
things. Like last night—maybe I wasn't the only person who heard someone running around at the time
of the robbery at the Garretts' house."

◆◆◆◆◆◆◆◆◆◆◆◆◆◆◆◆◆◆

CHOCOLATE BOOKS

The Emperors of Chocolate: Inside the Secret World of Hershey and Mars by *Joel Glenn Brenner* (RANDOM HOUSE)

Joel Glenn Brenner takes a look at the largest chocolate makers of the United States, Hershey and Mars, both conglomerates of mind-boggling size.

Her book outlines the history of each company and has a plot and cast of characters more interesting than most novels can boast. The leading actors are Milton Hershey, who built a giant company and then gave it away, and Forrest Mars Sr., who fought to found his own firm and then staged a takeover of the one his father had founded.

Interestingly enough, the book also includes succinct descriptions of growing and manufacturing chocolate that are among the best I've read.

Hersey developed his own recipe for chocolate, and the Hershey's bar created the American market for chocolate. But Hershey's never became popular in other parts of the world.

Mars developed chocolate products more in line with European standards and made M&M's the most popular candy in the United States.

◆◆◆◆◆◆◆◆◆◆◆◆◆◆◆◆◆◆

Chapter 9

That got my attention. Harold had heard someone running? Joe and I had been sure the burglars had taken off by boat.

"Running?" Joe said. "Where was this running?"

"On Lake Shore Drive. Coming from the stairs."

"The stairs down to Beech Tree Public Access Area?"

Harold nodded, and Joe went on. "Did you tell the police about this?"

"Sure. I told them last night. They had cops going up and down the beach and the road first thing this morning. I guess they figured like I did—the people who held you guys up ran along the beach and got away up the stairs."

"That's possible."

"But if the cops found anything, they didn't let on."

"I doubt they did find anything," Joe said. "It was too dry to leave tracks in the sand—tracks that could be identified, I mean. And I doubt any crook who ever watched television would be dumb enough to drop a button or a cigarette butt. The beach would be a pretty good escape route."

I thought about that while Joe and Harold talked a

few minutes longer. Harold was right about the beach being a good escape route. If the guys who had held us at gunpoint had run along the shore, they could have been at the public access area in about two minutes. Then they could have crossed to the stairs that swimmers took down to the beach, gone up to the small parking area, gotten into a car left there or in a nearby driveway, and driven off for points unknown. And they could have easily done it before the cops arrived.

Harold lingered until Joe's replies to him reached the monosyllable stage. It was Alice who finally showed signs of leaving. I could hear her snuffling around in the flower bed. Then she stood up on her hind feet and looked in the dining room window at me.

"Quit dancing around, Alice," Harold said.

Dancing. The word made me jump.

Dancing? Dancing? I felt the word was significant, but I didn't know why.

Another cup of coffee might help. I poured some caffeine from the thermal carafe into my mug, and sipped it. The dining room is tiled and the floor felt cold to my feet. *Lordy,* I thought, *no wonder my brain won't work. I don't even have my shoes on.*

Shoes. That did it. My blood got out of bed. My heart began to pound, and my brain began to race. When Joe came into the dining room, he faced a lively wife.

"Joe! I just realized something about that third burglar!"

"The guy who had been upstairs?"

"Right! He was wearing dance shoes!"

"Dance shoes? Ballet slippers?"

"No! I think they're called jazz shoes. They look like oxfords."

"When were you around men's dance shoes?"

"They're worn by women as well as men. Sometimes. Dancing lessons were part of my mom's attempt to turn me into a silk purse when she was grooming me for the pageant circuit."

"I knew you had dance lessons, but I pictured you as a little girl in a tutu."

"I started too late for ballet. I just had some simple movement classes. My mom thought it would miraculously make me graceful."

He grinned. "I guess it worked. You waft over the ground like a gazelle."

"More like a cow pony running through a rough pasture. But the lessons were helpful when I was doing all those pageants. Part of every competition is a big musical number to open the show, and all the contestants have to participate. The number had to be simple, of course, because some of us couldn't dance. And the others usually couldn't sing."

"And you wore men's dance shoes?"

"I wish! Usually we had to wear high heels, and they were picked for color, not comfort. But lots of the choreographers were men. And they had to teach this ungainly group to move around the stage with a reasonable amount of rhythm and grace, so they definitely did not plan a ballet number. No point work, no lifts, no high kicks. And no tap dancing, either. Therefore, the guys teaching us would wear jazz shoes."

Joe still looked puzzled, so I went on. "If you've seen male dancers perform, you've seen jazz shoes. And as I said, women dancers wear them for some numbers. The shoes look like oxfords, and they tie like oxfords. But they're more flexible than oxfords. They're soft."

"Ideal for burglars."

"Yes! They would be ideal. Remember how quietly that guy ran down the stairs and across the bare floor of the living room?" I rapped the table for emphasis. "Besides, I could see that bunion on his right foot, and a stiff oxford or even a pair of black leather tennis shoes probably would have hidden it. So I'm sure I'm right. He was wearing a pair of black jazz shoes!"

I heard a mew. That was the only word for it. It sounded like a cat in distress, and it was coming from the living room.

Before I could take the sound in, Gina came into the dining room. She was smiling oddly.

I stared at her. "Are you all right?"

"Of course. Why wouldn't I be?"

"What was that funny noise?"

"It may have been me. I turned my ankle, but it's nothing serious. Did I hear you talking about Capezios?"

"I mentioned jazz shoes. I suppose they could be Capezios. I don't know much about the brands. Why?"

"Oh. No reason." Gina walked on through the kitchen, apparently bound for the bathroom.

I turned to Joe. "Should I call the detectives and add that bit of observation to the statement I made last night?"

"Sure. You never know. Jazz shoes might fit the MO of some known burglar. And I've got to leave."

"I thought you and Darrell were going to work on the bathroom today."

"We were. But we've both gotten roped into the search for the home invaders."

"*The Search for the Home Invaders.* It sounds like a bad movie."

"I'm afraid it's not going to be that entertaining. The state police want the shore searched for several miles north and south of Double Diamond. I'm going to get out the boat, and Darrell and I will follow the shore from the river south to Double Diamond's beach, looking for anything interesting on the way. They've got other people asking around the docks, looking for boaters who were out last night."

"Then I guess they're not sold on the thieves escaping by running up the beach, the way Harold thinks they got away."

"No, they're checking out the boat angle, too. But our part of the search is a complete waste of time. Just routine."

"At least you won't be working in the bathroom, so I won't be in your way if I take another shower."

"Shower away. I hope Darrell and I can get back to the construction business this afternoon."

I got some bottled water out of the refrigerator for Joe and Darrell. I reminded Joe that this was my day off. Joe assured me that he had his cell phone and would call to tell me when they'd get home.

By the time I'd eaten a piece of toast, Gina had gone back upstairs. Before I cleared the table, I picked up the phone to call the Warner Pier PD and ask them who—if anybody—needed to know about the dance shoes. For a moment the phone didn't seem to be working right. Then I heard a click. I hung up and lifted the receiver again, and this time things seemed normal, so I punched in the right numbers.

However, my call to the Warner Pier PD wasn't very productive. The only person not out detecting like mad, apparently, was the dispatcher. She told me she'd pass the word along to someone.

Anyway, I'd done my duty, so I rinsed and stacked the breakfast dishes and put the toaster away. Then I called up to Gina, telling her I was getting into the shower. Not that I thought she'd answer the phone or wash the dishes while I was occupied.

Twenty minutes later I turned off the shower, then decided that—with only Gina and me in the house— I'd dry my hair and put on makeup in the bathroom. Because of the crowd of people using the partially disabled bathroom, I'd been doing my hair and makeup in the bedroom most of the time. But this time I thought—just as a special treat—I'd do that chore in the bathroom.

So, leaving the bathroom's exhaust fan on to clear the mirror, I wrapped my body in a big towel and my hair in a smaller one, and then went into the bedroom. I'd just picked up the dryer when I heard Gina's voice above my head.

"Thank you very much," she said briskly.

I stopped in midreach, my curiosity bug on alert. After two weeks of seclusion, Gina was talking to someone. Who? Was there someone upstairs?

I rejected that idea. Gina must be on the phone. That meant she was in the bedroom now occupied by Brenda and Tracy. It had been my room when I was living with Aunt Nettie, so the upstairs extension was there. In fact, she must have been on the phone when I picked it up earlier. That would explain the odd click and delayed dial tone.

Brenda and Tracy were out, and there was certainly no reason that Gina couldn't use the phone in their room if she wanted to, though I'd have expected her to come down and use the kitchen phone. But whom was she calling?

I was dying to know.

I didn't have to tap the phone line to find out. I just kept standing in the middle of my bedroom, with one ear cocked toward the ceiling. I hadn't turned on the fan in our bedroom, so if Gina said anything more, I'd be able to hear it.

And she did speak. "Hello," she said. "Do you have a Mr. Atkins registered?"

Registered, she'd said. Gina had called a hotel or motel.

I stood silently for thirty seconds or so. Then Gina spoke again. "No? How about an Andy Woodyard?"

Andy Woodyard! That was when I nearly dropped the hair dryer.

What the heck was going on? Andy Woodyard was Joe's dad's name. First a strange man came to the door claiming to be Joe's dad. Then Joe assured me there was no question that his father had actually been drowned thirty years earlier. And now Gina was calling motels trying to find her dead brother.

And Gina's ex—or soon-to-be ex—was named Atkins. He had the other name she'd asked for.

But I had thought she was hiding out at our house because she didn't want her husband to find her. So why was she calling motels trying to track him down?

I decided to storm up the stairs and demand an explanation.

Then I hesitated. The Andy Woodyard question had more to do with Joe than with me. Should I talk to Gina without talking to Joe first? Yes, I decided.

I almost headed straight for the stairs. Then I realized that I was wearing nothing but two towels, and the big one was slipping off my body, and the small one was falling off my head. If I went to confront Gina, it might be better not to do it naked and with wet hair stringing down my back.

I went back into the bathroom, dried myself off, and put on my clean underwear and my terry-cloth robe. Then I ran a comb through my wet hair and dried it enough to keep it from dripping. I took a deep breath and looked in the mirror, checking to be sure there was a resolute set to my jaw.

I was going to ask Gina what was going on. She might not answer me, true, but what was the worst that could happen? She might get mad and leave. I could always hope.

I jammed my feet into slippers and stalked toward the stairs, keeping up my resolution by reminding myself that this was my house—my honeymoon cottage—and too many things were happening in it that I didn't understand.

For example, Pete. Who was he? Knowing he was a former client of Joe's did nothing to recommend him.

And Darrell. Where did he fit in?

Why did Joe and Pete stop talking whenever I came into a room? Why had they been holed up in Darrell's camper for at least an hour Monday night, just talking?

I might not be able to answer any of those questions, but at least I could ask Gina why she'd been calling motels looking for her dead brother and her ex-husband. And maybe finding out the answer to that would lead to answers to a few other questions, starting with what the heck she was doing in my house, anyway.

"Gina!" I called out as I went up the stairs, and I was surprised when she didn't answer.

"Gina!" I called again at the top of the stairs. Still no answer.

I went on down the hall. Gina's door was closed, and when I reached it, I stopped. Did I really want to risk an argument with Joe's aunt?

I reminded myself that Gina was acting very oddly, that this was my house, and I had a right to know what she was up to. More than a right—a responsibility.

I squared my shoulders, took a deep breath, and knocked on the door. "Gina?"

Still no answer.

I pushed the door open and looked into the room.

There were the old maple bed and dresser that had belonged to my great-grandparents. The casement windows were open, and the red-and-blue-plaid curtains were pushed back. The bed was neatly made, its navy blue spread unwrinkled. The romance novels I'd checked out from the Warner Pier Library were stacked on the bedside table.

The only thing missing was Gina.

Maybe she was in the girls' room, still beside the phone.

I turned to that room, which was across the hall from Gina's, and looked in the open door. The room wasn't as messy as I'd feared, since eighteen-year-olds have much more important things to worry about than neatness. The bed was made, or at least the spread had been pulled up. There were clothes on the chairs and on the foot of the bed, true, but none on the floor. Belts, bras, and necklaces dangled from the handle of the closet door. The telephone sat on the bedside table.

There was no sign of Gina here either.

I couldn't believe it. I looked in the closet, feeling silly, then went back to Gina's room and looked in that closet. I considered getting down on my knees and looking under the beds in both rooms.

I was standing in the hall, feeling stupid, when I had another idea.

"She must be downstairs," I told myself. "She probably went down while I had the hair dryer on."

I ran down myself. "Gina!"

Still no answer.

Quickly I looked through the house. There aren't that many rooms. Living room, dining room, kitchen, downstairs bedroom, back hall, bathroom. I looked in all of them. I even went downstairs to our Michigan basement—a cellar with concrete walls and a sand floor.

Gina wasn't anywhere.

I was absolutely amazed.

For a week Gina had kept to the house, refusing to leave or even to talk on the phone. She had done nothing but lie on her bed reading romance novels. She had barely appeared for meals and had hidden if anyone came to the door.

And now she had not only made some phone calls; she had even left the house.

Where the heck had she gone?

Chapter 10

I was so amazed by Gina's disappearance that I almost called the cops. Then I imagined how stupid I'd sound.

I wanted to have a serious talk with my houseguest, I'd tell them, but when I looked for her I discovered she'd gone out for a walk.

Big whoop.

That was the reason people came to Warner Pier, after all. They wanted to get out in the fresh air and go to the beach and look at the beautiful scenery. Just because Gina hadn't done that for the first week of her visit didn't mean she wouldn't ever do it.

So I didn't call for help. I made my bed, then dressed in denim shorts, a T-shirt, and tennis shoes, telling myself that Gina would reappear momentarily. But when I came out of the bedroom, Gina hadn't come back. So I went outside to look for her.

I circled the house, calling her name every now and then. Not too loudly. I didn't want to be hollering all over the neighborhood. Gina might still be hiding out, even though she'd gone outside. Maybe Gina had come down with an acute case of cabin fever. I knew I would have been climbing the walls if I'd been in one room as much as she had.

The ground was still damp from the rain in the night. When I reached our driveway, I could see clear footprints in the sandy surface. I decided to see if they told me anything. I felt silly looking at the ground like some kind of frontier tracker, but I couldn't think of anything else to do.

There were plenty of tracks to look at.

The girls had stomped around in their tennis shoes as they got into Brenda's car to go to work. Darrell's steel-toed boots were easy to spot; they led to his camper. Okay, I admit it—I tried the door of the camper. I would have loved a peek inside, but it was locked.

Then there were tracks of two sets of men's tennis shoes, one slightly larger than the other. I assumed one was Joe and the other was Pete, especially after I noted that the slightly larger shoes stopped where Pete's SUV had been parked, and the shorter shoes went off down the back drive toward the Baileys' house, where Joe and I had both been parking, since our own drive was crammed full. Darrell's boots followed along, occasionally stepping on top of Joe's tennies, so I could tell he'd been walking behind.

I'd noticed earlier that Harold Glick wore crepe-soled shoes, so his tracks were easy to spot. Of course, I couldn't miss Alice's pawprints, and she was always right beside him. Besides, I knew they'd walked up the drive and around to our back door earlier.

It was in the drive that I found the first evidence of where Gina had gone—the prints of a high-heeled shoe.

I followed the tracks for ten or twelve feet. Gina

had been going down the back drive, toward the Baileys' house. Once or twice she'd stepped on top of Joe's tracks.

Then her tracks changed dramatically. Abruptly, instead of high-heeled shoes tripping along, there were the prints of bare feet. Then those disappeared.

I stopped and stared. I could understand Gina kicking her shoes off; they were probably getting sand in them. But the barefoot tracks stopped right in the middle of the drive. They simply evaporated. Had Gina been yanked up by a balloon? Picked up by a helicopter? Snagged by a noose and thrown into the top of a tree?

I even looked up suspiciously. Right at that spot, tall maples hung over the road. I suppose Gina could have been pulled straight up by some sort of apparatus, but I saw no sign of it. I shook myself. I was getting silly. So I looked at the ground again. I saw some pits in the surface of the drive. I knelt and looked at them closely.

Then I saw that the impressions of toes edged the pits. The "pits" I'd seen had been the balls of Gina's feet. She'd been walking along on tiptoe.

"Tiptoeing? Gina was tiptoeing?" I was so amazed that I think I spoke aloud.

However she was traveling, Gina had still been headed toward the Baileys' house. Feeling like some sort of big game hunter, I kept following her tracks. I followed them until the tiptoe prints reached the Baileys' carport.

And that was the end. The Baileys' carport had a concrete floor. I found a few dustings of sand, but if Gina had tiptoed into the carport, all evidence of her had disappeared.

"Gina?" I said her name aloud, but there was no response.

The Baileys' house—a nondescript 1950s structure—
was empty for the moment, since Charlie and Mary
Bailey were in California. Which was why Joe and I
were able to use their drive for extra parking.

But Gina seemed to have tiptoed into their carport
and disappeared from our dimension. And she'd done
it in less than the ten or fifteen minutes I took to dry
my hair, put on a robe, and go up to her room.

I looked around the carport. There was simply no
place for Gina to hide. No closets, no toolshed, no big
bushes. The biggest thing in the carport was a bushel
basket I knew held gardening paraphernalia—ragged
gloves, a rusty trowel, some worn flip-flops, an old
piece of foam Charlie knelt on when he weeded the
flower beds, and other stuff. I ignored that and walked
around the house. Gina wasn't behind it. I tried the
doors. They were all locked.

Joe and I had a key, since we were the neighbors
designated to keep an eye on the place. Should I get
it and look inside?

But if Gina were hiding inside—and I had no idea
how she could have gotten in without leaving some
sign, such as a broken window or a jimmied lock—
she must have seen me wandering around in the yard.
She surely would have come to the door and waved
at me.

I walked south on the drive that led from the Baileys' house to Eighty-eighth Street. That street ran
east-to-west. It was surfaced with gravel, and it inter-
sected with Lake Shore Drive about an eighth of a
mile south of our drive. Lake Shore Drive, Eighty-
eighth Street, the Baileys' drive, and our drive formed
a rough square.

There were no more of Gina's footprints—bare,
high-heeled, tiptoe, or otherwise—on that end of the
drive. The only neighbors who seemed to have walked

along there were Harold and Alice. For a moment I considered going by Harold's house and asking him if he'd seen Gina. But Gina had always fled upstairs if Harold came by; I didn't like the idea of letting him know anything about her.

I reached Eighty-eighth Street, still searching for tracks like a frontier hunter. Of course, Eighty-eighth was a public street and led to several houses and a small subdivision east of us, so there was more traffic on it. Besides, the gravel surface wouldn't show the tracks of anything lighter than a loaded dump truck. I walked on to Lake Shore Drive, which is paved with asphalt. I saw no sign of Gina. I checked for tracks in the damp earth along the edge of the blacktop—staying clear of the occasional passing car—until I reached our drive. The only tracks I saw were a few wide, flat ones, the kind instantly recognizable as made by beach sandals. I didn't think Brenda even owned a pair of those; plus these particular ones must have belonged to a tall man with big feet. I wrote them off as belonging to some beachgoer.

I got back to the house without finding another hint of what had happened to Gina.

With a sort of desperation, I called her name again as I came in the door. No answer. A quick check, upstairs and down, confirmed that she had not returned while I was roaming around looking for her.

By now my stomach was in a knot. Where had she gone? What had happened to her?

The situation might not require the police, but I decided it was definitely odd enough for a call to Joe.

His cell phone rang several times before he answered, and then his words were terse. Or his word was terse.

"Yes."

"Joe?"

"I'll call you back." He broke the connection.

I made some guttural sound that signified frustration. "How can you hang up?" I asked the phone. "Gina is *your* aunt, not mine!"

Then I reminded myself that Joe was out in a boat, though I hadn't heard the motor. He might be facing some serious situation—bailing madly because there was a hole in the bottom maybe, or on a collision course with a big yacht.

"He'd better be facing a life-or-death situation," I said aloud. "If he isn't now, he will be when he gets home."

I debated calling him back. But then I had another idea. I went to the desk in the corner of the bedroom and dug around until I found a scrap of paper. "Aha!" I held it up.

Pete's cell, the scrap of paper read. Some scrawled numbers followed.

Since Pete seemed to know so much more about what was going on in my house than I did, I'd call him.

He answered on the second ring, and at first he sounded as terse as Joe had. But he let me tell him why I'd called.

I was feeling silly by the time I came to the end of my story. "So she might have simply gone out for a walk," I said lamely. "I may be panicking over nothing."

"I don't think so," Pete said. "I'll come help look for her."

I felt relieved at his answer. Unfortunately, he'd hung up without telling me where he was, so I had no idea how long it would take for him to get to the house. I was quite excited when a car drove in from Lake Shore Drive about ten minutes after I'd hung up, and I felt quite let down when Brenda and Tracy got out of it.

"Hey, Lee," Tracy said. "We're both broke. Do you mind if we fix ourselves a sandwich?"

"Go ahead," I said. "You didn't see Gina walking down Lake Shore Drive, did you?"

Both girls popped their eyes, and Brenda yelled in astonishment, "Gina went out?"

I shushed them quickly and sent them to the kitchen to make their own sandwiches. My stomach was so full of knots that I couldn't consider eating. Besides, it was only eleven thirty a.m. I stood on the front porch watching for Pete. But he didn't come.

It began to drizzle rain again. I was almost glad. If Gina was simply out walking around, surely she'd head for the house when she began to get wet. But she didn't show up.

I tried calling Joe again. He'd turned his phone off. Or maybe he'd dropped it in the lake. Or maybe he'd fallen in himself.

I couldn't think of anything else to do, so I went back out on the front porch and stood there looking out into the drizzle, sweating and wringing my hands.

Just then Darrell came walking down the drive, coming from the direction of the Baileys' house.

Darrell had left with Joe a couple of hours earlier. If he was back, then Joe was back. A sense of relief flooded me.

"Joe!" I passed Darrell without a nod and ran up the drive toward the Baileys' house. Joe and Darrell had apparently come in the back way and parked over there.

Joe's blue truck was parked in the Baileys' drive, but there was no sign of Joe himself.

For a minute I couldn't figure it out; if Darrell was there, where was Joe? Then I realized that Joe must have sent Darrell home in the truck and had himself stayed with the boat. But why?

I could ask Darrell. I turned around and started back down the sandy lane to our house. And now I thought about Gina's tracks. Had I ruined them in my headlong dash to the Baileys'? Had the drizzle destroyed them?

No, I found the tiptoe tracks still visible. But there were new marks beside them. Blunt semicircles had been dug in. What were they? For a moment I stared blankly. Then I looked at my own shoe. The blunt semicircles matched the toes of my shoes. But where was the rest of the track? Why had only the toes made a mark?

It was because I'd been running.

I compared my tracks to Gina's. They were nothing alike, of course. Hers were from bare feet, and I'd been wearing tennis shoes. The single similarity was that only the toes had made marks.

"Oh, lordy!" I said. "Gina wasn't tiptoeing! She was running!"

What could have happened to make Gina not only leave our house, but run down the drive toward the neighbor's carport?

I definitely needed to tell Joe about this. And I wanted him to see those tracks.

I whirled and ran back to the Baileys'. It took me only a moment to get a tarp from the back of Joe's truck. I spread it over the damp sand, covering the patch of ground that held Gina's tracks. Then I went to our front door, opened it, and yelled at Brenda and Tracy, "Come out here on the porch and eat your sandwiches, please!"

They stared. "It's wet out there." Tracy sounded incredulous.

"I know, but I need you to stop tragedy. I mean, traffic! I don't want any cars to drive over that tarp."

I guess my excitement convinced them that my request was important. They came out and sat in the porch chairs, eating their sandwiches and looking confused. I explained that they were to stop any vehicles from driving over the tarp I'd spread out.

I ran around the house to Darrell's camper and banged on the door. "Darrell! I have to find Joe. Where is he?"

Darrell didn't answer. I almost decided he hadn't gone inside when I heard a sniffle. He was there.

"Darrell! Why did Joe send you home? Where is he?"

Still no answer.

"Listen, Darrell, I've got an emergency here. I need Joe. It's vital! I have to reach him. And he's got his phone turned off. So, where is he and what's happened to him?"

I heard Darrell again, but he didn't answer.

"Darrell! Answer me!"

He didn't.

"Then I'll have to call the police department!" I turned away and flounced toward the house.

As I got to the back porch, the phone rang. I ran inside, letting the door slam behind me. But Tracy had gotten there first.

"Hi, Gina," she said. "How're you doin'?"

"Give me that!" I snatched the phone away from her. "Gina! Where are you?"

"That doesn't matter. But I wanted you to know I'm all right."

"Thank God! You scared me. Shall I come and get you?"

"No, no! I think I'd better stay where I am for a while."

"Gina! Where are you?"

"I'm in a safe place, hon. Now don't worry."

She hung up.

Chapter 11

I growled and stared at the telephone. I would have liked to use it to bop Gina on the head.

Why hadn't we gotten caller ID? But if Gina was using her cell phone and didn't want to talk, knowing the number wouldn't help me, anyway.

At that point Pete drove up. I was so glad to see a person who seemed to be taking me seriously, who shared my concern about Gina—even Pete—that I had to fight the impulse to run to his SUV, haul him out, and hug the male chauvinist pig. I think I maintained proper decorum only because he saw that Brenda and Tracy were trying to get out of the drive—by then it was time for them to go back to work. He started to go past our drive to the Baileys' house, and he almost ran over the tarp. So I ran out yelling, but I didn't hug him. I signaled for him to stop.

Pete had to back clear out to Lake Shore Drive to let the girls out. By the time he had parked in his usual spot I had my emotions under control.

"Finally!" I said. "Finally I've got someone to look at these tracks. Though it may not be as important now as it was a half hour ago."

I told Pete about Gina's phone call. He listened seriously, but all he said was, "I'll take a look at the tracks, since you've preserved them."

Naturally, it then began to rain in earnest and the sky grew as dark as a Jamaican Rum Truffle ("the ultimate dark chocolate truffle"). I got a flashlight, and Pete and I held the tarp up like a floppy tent and he looked at the tracks. We both got muddy. And hot. The rain hadn't cooled anything off.

"So Gina wouldn't say where she was," he said.

"No! Somebody must have picked her up."

"She's not being held prisoner if she can get to a phone."

"Unless someone forced her to call."

Pete nodded. He was still concentrating on the ground. "Can you hold the tarp by yourself?"

"Maybe."

I tried, but my attempt wasn't very successful. Pete squatted down, and we draped the tarp over his back, leaving his rump out in the rain. I stood up with my arms held out in front, doing my impression of tent poles, while Pete ducked down. Then Pete suddenly stood up, and the two of us were nose-to-nose.

Maybe if I hadn't been so mad at Joe I wouldn't have noticed our closeness.

Pete backed up slightly. "I don't know a lot about tracks," he said. "But it does look as if Gina was running."

"Is it worth calling the police about?" I asked.

"I don't think we could report her as a missing person until she's been gone longer. Not after that phone call."

We were still standing there, still nose-to-nose, when I heard Joe laugh.

"What the heck are you two doing?" he said. "You look like an amateur show elephant."

I dropped my hands, and the tarp slipped off to one side. The next thing I knew I had grabbed Joe in a stranglehold that nearly kept him from breathing. Joe held me for a long moment.

Rain was running down my neck. "Darn, Joe!" I said. "You startled me so much I forgot I was mad at you."

"What were you mad about?"

I let go of him. "It's a long story. Get Pete to tell you. I'll go in the house and make some sandwiches. You *experts* decide what to do about Gina."

"Gina?" Joe's voice was puzzled. I didn't answer.

Joe and Pete stood out in the rain, and I could see Pete gesturing toward the ground, so I gathered that he did tell Joe about the big Gina chase. But they apparently decided to do nothing, because when I looked out the window they had folded the tarp up and were heading toward the house.

By then I'd determined that I'd act absolutely normal with Pete. I'd treat him strictly as Joe's friend. That was the ticket. It was just so weird to find myself attracted to a man I'd have sworn I didn't even like, a man I'd described as reminding me of my ex-husband.

Of course, at one time I'd been very strongly attracted to Rich or I wouldn't have married him.

I met Joe and Pete at the front door. "Y'all might as well talk to Darrell before you come in," I said. "As if we didn't have enough perversity—I mean personality! If we didn't have enough personality conflicts around here, Darrell has locked himself in his camper, and he wouldn't answer when I knocked."

Joe and Pete did their wordless communication act. Then Joe sighed. "I'll go."

"See if he'll come in to lunch," I said.

Joe plodded off around the house, and Pete came inside, wiping his feet on a rug near the door.

"What is Darrell's problem, anyway?" I said.

"He's had a lot of rough breaks, with his dad and all."

"His dad?"

Pete rolled his eyes. "I guess Joe hasn't told you about Darrell's dad."

"No. But I hope you will."

"When Darrell was twelve years old, his dad was beating his mom. Darrell got involved. His dad wound up dead with a butcher knife in his side."

"How horrible! Did Darrell stab him? Or was it his mom?"

"No one really knows. Even Darrell may not know. The scene had turned into a melee. But Darrell was the one who got the knife from the kitchen and told his dad to back off. He was never charged."

"I should think not!"

Pete smiled cynically. "Things aren't always as simple as they sound."

"Do you think it was deliberate?"

"I'm not saying that. But whatever happened, a thing like that's going to leave a mark."

I went back to the kitchen and got out some lettuce for the sandwiches. As I drained it on paper towels, I tried to calm down the emotions that the account of Darrell's involvement in his father's death had brought out. I may have blinked back a couple of tears.

What a sad, sad thing to happen to a twelve-year-old kid. But as Pete said, there are a lot of ramifications to crime—particularly crimes within a family. Who knows what had really happened?

But Darrell had faced a lot in less than twenty-five years of life. His own involvement—justified or not—in his father's death; then wrongful conviction for a home invasion and a resulting death; then five years in prison. And he'd apparently coped with it all by retreating within himself and learning to hide his emotions.

No wonder Darrell always made me feel nervous. He must have a bomb inside his head. Ticking. There had to be oceans of emotion inside his stoic exterior. He needed some way to let it out.

Darrell came in the back door, his head hanging. He wore a cap that left his drab hair sticking out around the edges. Joe's hand was on his shoulder.

"Lunch is almost ready," I said. I hoped my voice sounded normal.

Joe nudged Darrell toward the bathroom, and he shuffled off, the picture of defeat.

At lunch Joe had me go over Gina's disappearance again. I described how I'd found that she wasn't in her room, then searched the house and the immediate neighborhood for her. Darrell ignored us. He made himself a sandwich, but he ate it staring at his plate.

Joe frowned. "Why did you go upstairs to talk to her in the first place?"

"To find out about the calls to motels."

Joe and Pete looked at me with completely blank expressions.

"Motels?" Joe sounded puzzled.

"Didn't I tell Pete about that? I heard her upstairs. The fan was on in the bathroom, so I guess she thought I was still in there. She was in the girls' room using the telephone, and you know this house; I could hear every word she said."

Joe frowned, and he and Pete exchanged one of those significant stares.

Pete gave a snort of disgust. "We should have thought of that," he said.

"If we'd known who to ask for," Joe said.

"That was the funny part," I said. "Gina was looking for relatives."

"Relatives?"

"Yes. First she asked for Mr. Atkins."

"Atkins!" Joe dropped his fork.

"Yes. Wasn't that her ex-husband's name?"

"Did she ask for Art Atkins?"

"I think she just asked for Mr. Atkins. No first name. But Gina spent all this time avoiding him. Why would she be trying to find him now?"

"I don't know," Joe said.

I shrugged. "I guess she might need to talk to him for some legal reason. It was the second name she asked for that caught my attention."

"Who was it?"

"Andy Woodyard."

Joe stared at me blankly. Then his mouth grew tight. "This is getting old," he said. "Who is this guy? And if Gina knew something about him, why didn't she say so?"

"If you mean the man who came to the door claiming to be your dad, I don't think I ever mentioned him to Gina," I said. "She didn't know about his visit, unless you told her."

Joe slammed a fist on the table. "When I think of the length of time it took for me to realize that my dad was actually gone forever, the times I dreamed he came in the front door, and I said, 'I thought you were dead,' and he answered, 'No, I'm alive. . . .' "

I heard a huge gasp coming from Darrell's side of the table. We all stared at him. Tears were welling in his eyes. He half rose from the table, looking panicky.

Joe grabbed his arm. "It's okay, Darrell."

Darrell rapidly blinked. "I thought I was the only person who had that dream," he said.

"Hell!" Pete said. "I have it, and my dad died of a heart attack at the age of seventy-five."

That killed the conversation for a few minutes, but Darrell sat down again, and we all took a few deep breaths.

I turned to Pete, searching madly for some less emotionally charged subject to bring up. I didn't think Joe and Darrell wanted the lunch table to turn into a therapy session.

"Was your dad an outdoor type, Pete? Is that how you got interested in birds?"

"Nope," Pete said. "He served thirty years in the navy. The only bird he ever watched was a seagull."

That didn't get a general laugh—Joe was too uptight, and Darrell was still looking tearful—but the atmosphere lightened up. After all three guys had finished their sandwiches and cookies, and had each indulged in a few pieces of the molded chocolates, still tasty if they were a bit misshapen from the heat, Joe asked Darrell if he wanted to work on the shelves at the TenHuis Chocolade that afternoon.

"It's an inside job," he said. "There's not much to do at the boat shop, it looks like it's going to keep raining, and all the work on the bathroom addition is outside."

"Sure," Darrell said. He cut his eyes at me, then looked at Joe as he got to his feet. "Sure. I'll get started."

"I'd better check with Dolly," I said. "Things are a mess down there because of the air-conditioning problems."

Sure enough, Dolly said Cal Vandemann had not shown up, though his mom had called to say he might have located a compressor. In Illinois. It would be difficult for Darrell to work in the storeroom where the shelves were to go, she said, because that was one of the few cool places in the plant.

"I've got the cases of jewel boxes for that Indianapolis gift shop stored in there," she said. "Plus the latest shipment of chocolate."

So I had to tell Darrell it wasn't a good time for him to work on the shelves.

Joe immediately came up with an alternate plan. "You can go to the lumberyard in Holland," he said. "I'll make a list for there and for Smith's Boat Supply."

He made the list quickly and gave Darrell the keys to his truck. As Darrell left I caught Pete sending Joe one of those significant looks I resented. Pete stood up. "I'll volunteer to do the dishes," he said.

"Pete, I can do that," I said. I like help around the house, but I don't like strange bird-watchers messing around in my kitchen. They hide things, and heaven knows how a macho type like Pete would do dishes.

Joe took my hand. "Let Pete do it," he said. "He's fairly sanitary, and I need to talk to you."

All the significant looks had annoyed me. I pulled my hand away from Joe, leaned back in my chair, and folded my arms across my chest. "Are you going to let me in on whatever the heck is going on around here?"

Joe frowned. "What do you mean?"

"You and Pete, and sometimes Darrell, are always exchanging these looks that seem to be fraught with meaning. And whenever I ask what's going on, y'all say I'm imagining things."

"In this case it's more a matter of breaking it to you gently," Joe said. "The searchers found a body this morning."

"Who is it?"

"We don't know, Lee. But the state police detective thinks it might be one of the robbers from last night. He wants both of us to take a look at him."

I guess I didn't look very pleased at that prospect,

because Joe patted my arm reassuringly. "They say he doesn't look too bad."

"Then you've seen him?"

"No." Joe smiled. "And I'm not supposed to tell you anything. Van Dam wants your unprejudiced opinion. Will you do it?"

"Of course."

"We need to get going then. The state police are holding the body here until we've had a chance to see it."

Joe was completely silent as he drove me to the Warner Pier Funeral Home, where the man who'd been pulled from the lake was temporarily in residence.

Detective Sergeant Larry Underwood, of the Michigan State Police, was sitting in the funeral home office. When we came in, he hastily stuffed the remnants of a sandwich into a Sidewalk Café sack and stood up.

Underwood had moved up the ranks since Joe and I had met him a couple of years earlier. He still had a blocky build, and his buzz cut was just as black as ever. He was just a little shorter than I am, but who wasn't?

"We appreciate your coming, Lee," he said. "The guy doesn't look too bad."

"I've seen dead people before," I said. If I sounded a bit tart, it was probably because all this solicitousness from Joe and now from Underwood was beginning to give me the jimjams. "Let's get it over with."

Underwood led the way into what I suppose was the cold room of the funeral home. A long shape lay on one of the tables, covered by a sheet.

Underwood went to the head and gently lifted the sheet.

"I didn't see the face of any of the robbers," I said. "I might do better looking at this guy's feet."

"Take a look at the face anyway," Underwood said. "Does he look familiar?" He pulled the sheet back, revealing a shock of hair, then a face.

For a minute I was too surprised to answer. I clutched Joe's arm.

Joe gave me his left hand and slid the right one around me. "Do you recognize him, Lee?"

"Joe! It's that guy who said he was your dad!"

Chapter 12

"**A**re you sure?"

That was Joe's first question, of course. But I *was* sure. And as I pointed out the reasons, all Joe could do was nod.

"The gray hair, the scar on the cheek," I said. "I can't tell how tall he is, and he's not smiling, but I'm sure it's the guy."

Larry Underwood was frowning. "This is Joe's dad?"

"No!" I barked the word out, surprised that Joe didn't reply even more quickly than I did.

Then I quickly filled Underwood in on the unexpected arrival of a person claiming to be Joe's dad—returned from the grave.

Underwood scowled. "Then this guy is not one of the robbers?"

"I have no idea," I said. "They were completely disguised. He could have been one of them. Let's take a look at his feet."

Underwood uncovered the other end of the body, revealing a large pair of masculine feet. Feet in general aren't particularly beautiful, what with toes going

off at angles and strange calluses and odd-looking toe-
nails, but these feet were neat, if not attractive. They
were slender and well shaped, and the nails were
trimmed.

And on the right foot was a large bunion.

I pointed to it. "I guess that's not proof," I said,
"but the robber who ran down from upstairs did have
a bunion large enough to be visible in the soft shoes
he wore."

"It's sure a funny coincidence if he wasn't one of
the robbers." Underwood turned to Joe. "Do you recognize him?"

Joe said the man's face didn't look familiar to him,
and he hadn't noticed the robber's foot. Then Underwood told somebody they could take the body to
the medical examiner, and he escorted Joe and me
down to the Warner Pier PD to be interviewed. Because, of course, the idea of a strange man coming to
the door and claiming to be Joe's dad one day and
turning up dead a couple of days later was, as he'd
said, "a funny coincidence."

"Too funny to laugh at," Joe said. "Underwood,
have you run prints on this guy?"

"We're in the process."

"Maybe you should check your records and see if
you have prints for an Art Atkins."

"Gina's ex?" I blurted the words out.

Joe nodded.

"Did he have a record?" I asked.

"Not that I know of, but I'm beginning to wonder."
Joe turned to Underwood. "This guy who came to the
door—he's got to have some connection with my family; at least, he knows some member of it. That's the
only way he could know who my dad was and that he
died when I was so young that I wouldn't know what
he looked like. And my aunt's ex-husband is one per-

son I can think of who might fit that role. If it was him, it might begin to explain why she seems to be afraid of the guy.''

''Surely Gina wasn't married to a cricket—I mean, a criminal!'' I was horrified.

''I'm not so sure,'' Joe said. ''Art Atkins had her on the run, Lee. He still does, maybe. She's scared of him. And Gina's not one to back off from confrontation. This is something more than an argument over who gets the dishes.''

At this point Underwood began to ask questions, and Joe gave him background on Gina—background I hadn't known.

His aunt Gina—Regina Woodyard—had long operated a successful antique business, Joe said. She ran a shop in her hometown, with the help of a couple of employees, and also dealt over the Internet, specializing in antique costume jewelry. Of course, I'd learned that from Alex Gold.

Her marital history was checkered. ''She got out of the habit of taking a new name with every husband,'' Joe said. ''In fact, back when I was in law school I advised her not to do that. She simply trades them in too fast. I think Atkins was number five.''

And he hadn't been kidding, Joe assured me, when he said that Gina met her most recent ex-husband at a family reunion. He was a third cousin to Gina and to Joe's dad.

''He might be a relative,'' he told Underwood. ''If you count that far back. One of the things that makes me wonder if this guy is Art Atkins is that Lee said his smile was sort of like mine. And my mom has always said that even though I look more like her family than like my dad's, I do have his smile. And once when I got stubborn about something, my dad's mother said I had the Atkins jaw. She meant I looked pigheaded, but it could have been something about the mouth and jaw muscles, I guess."

Gina and Art Atkins had been married for a year or so, but Joe had never met him.

"I try to go see my grandmother every couple of months," he said. "But I deliberately check on her when Gina's out of town. Not because I don't like Gina, but because that's when my grandmother might need a family member around. Anyway, I just never happened to cross paths with Gina's latest. Gina said he traveled a lot. Apparently he was also in the antique business. He went to a lot of sales and auctions, or so he told her."

The three of us raised our eyebrows at that. *Sales and auctions* might be code words for *burglary and theft* when it came to explaining where Atkins had picked up his antiques.

The main thing our talk with Underwood accomplished, from my point of view, was to alert the police that Gina was missing. Or that in my opinion she was missing. Since she was an adult who had been gone only a few hours—and who had called to say she was all right—she definitely wasn't a missing person from the law enforcement standpoint. But if—as Joe suspected—the man found in the lake that morning turned out to be her ex-husband . . . well, Underwood was going to have even more funny coincidences. There had to be a connection to her sudden departure.

Joe didn't go into one of the other coincidences around our house—namely Pete the bird-watcher. I asked him about this on our way home, but his answers were absentminded. I finally got his attention by telling him that Pete had told me about Darrell's involvement in his father's death.

"Yeah," Joe said. "Darrell has a tragic background.

I guess that's why he got so upset when he saw the body."

"You said you didn't see it."

"I'd gone into the office there at the marina when they lifted the body out onto the dock. But Darrell was still sitting in the boat. And one of the divers yelped out, 'He's been stabbed.' When I came out, Darrell was shaking all over. So I told him I'd get a ride from one of the cops and sent him back to the house."

"The dead man was stabbed?"

"That's what the diver said. Underwood didn't say anything about a cause of death. But it wouldn't be surprising. Thieves fall out."

When we got home, Joe went to the boat shop. Pete was gone, leaving a pile of dishes teetering in the drainer.

I sat down then, and I realized that I was alone, and I could do anything I wanted to do.

So I called Garnet Garrett.

That may seem like a strange thing to do. True, she'd entertained Joe and me for dinner the night before, and the custom along the lakeshore was the same as most other places. The phone call of thanks has largely replaced the thank-you note, but some expression of appreciation to a hostess is still a convention.

I practiced saying, "You gave us an unforgettable evening," with a straight face. But while the evening might have been unforgettable—and terrifying—to me, it had been a severe financial loss to Garnet, if her uncle Alex had used the stolen jewelry for collateral for a loan. If he'd wiped out the nest egg she and Dick had needed to get their son through medical school debt-free, Garnet might have spent the day crying her eyes out.

But I wanted to talk to her. First, I needed to make sure she knew Joe and I didn't blame her in any way for the scary experience we'd had. Second, I was dying to know if she'd noticed anything about the three robbers that I hadn't.

Garnet had given me her phone number, but I'd apparently left it at the office. I got the number from information and punched it in. Uncle Alex answered.

"I'm sorry, Mrs. Woodyard," he said formally. "Garnet and Dick have gone home to Grand Rapids."

"Please tell her that I'm sorry those bad guys interrupted her lovely dinner party. We were having such a good time! How are you taking it all, Mr. Gold?"

"With a deep sense of guilt, I'm afraid."

"You mustn't blame yourself!"

"But I do. I've carried valuable jewelry all over the United States and have never had a problem. I got overconfident."

I made a few soothing comments, then asked when Garnet and Dick would be back.

"Not for a few days," Alex said.

"Then you're alone?"

Alex paused. "Yes, but it's fine."

I felt awful. Garnet must be really mad at her uncle to have gone off and left him on his own. "Please come over to our house and take potluck tonight," I said. "We're not having anything elaborate, but we'd love to have you."

Alex cleared his throat. "That's very kind, Mrs. Woodyard, but I've already planned to treat myself to my favorite dinner. I'll tell Garnet that you called. Good-bye."

He hung up, leaving me still undecided about just what to do next.

Had I really had the nerve to invite Alex Gold to

dinner? I didn't even know what we were going to have.

That thought brought me back to earth after the emotional highs and lows of the past twenty-four hours. My Texas grandmother never got up from the table after one meal without knowing what she'd be serving at the next. When I'd teased her about this, as a twelve-year-old, she'd firmly said that good meals didn't just appear on the table. They took planning.

I could feel her frowning at me from some heavenly vantage point. I had all these houseguests, and they'd received only "bought" food and no entertainment. I got out my recipe collection and started through it.

Pot roast was out. It was too hot to cook it, and it took too long. The same objection eliminated stew; besides, the gang had had something similar to stew within the past couple of days. It looked like meat loaf night. We could stand the oven for an hour. It was so hot already that no one would notice.

I checked the refrigerator, made a list, and pulled out of the driveway with every intention of going straight to the Superette to pick up three pounds of ground round and seven baking potatoes. But for some reason I went out the back way and got sidetracked.

Leaving that way took me past the little gray house where my friend Inez Deacon used to live. Now that Inez was in a retirement center, that house was rented to Harold Glick and his dog, Alice. While I had early rejected asking Harold if he'd seen Gina, Harold did see every darn thing that happened in our neighborhood. Maybe there was some way I could ask him about Gina without asking him about Gina. Which shows how much sense I was making.

By then I'd stopped in Harold's driveway, and Alice

was running to the fence to greet me. There was no help for it. I had to get out of the van and go to the door. I opened my umbrella and went to the gate. Alice frisked around, yapping madly, while I edged inside the yard.

Once I had the gate closed behind me, I knelt and greeted her. "Hello, Alice. Nice to see you, too." She let me rub her behind the ears and scratch between her eyes.

I heard the door to the house open, and Harold spoke. "You know what she likes." He'd come out on the little front porch.

"All dogs like that," I said. "Sorry to drop in on you, but I had one quibble. I mean, question! I wanted to ask you something."

Harold closed the door behind him and stood at the top of the stairs. "Of course." He looked at me expectantly. I had to come up with a question, and I wasn't sure how to phrase it.

I killed time by walking over to stand right in front of Harold. It was still drizzling, and I almost joined him under his porch roof. I could hear his window air-conditioning unit whirring, and I had an impulse to push inside to get a whiff of cool air. He didn't invite me to do that, however. I stood in the yard and looked up at him from under my umbrella.

"Those guys you saw last night," I said. "How many were there?"

"I didn't actually see anybody, Lee. I heard them."

"What exactly did you hear?"

"The state police detective asked me that same question, and it's hard to explain. All I know is that I did feel sure that someone was running up the road. There were at least two of them. I heard feet pounding, and I think they must have been panting."

"That makes sense, if they'd been on the beach. . . .

Running in sand is one of the most adamant—I mean, arduous! It's arduous—a really hard thing to do." I went on quickly, trying not to give Harold any time to think about how stupid my remark had been. "But about your idea for a neighborhood watch—have you thought any more about that?"

"I haven't done anything. I think we'd have to register with the city, have membership meetings and such. Do you think it's a good idea?"

"It could be. All neighbors should look out for one another. But this area is so full of summer rentals, I'm not sure how it would work out. I mean, I see some really strange people walking up this road sometimes. You know, outfits that have to be seen to be believed! Some people apparently leave their fashion sense behind when they go on vacation!"

I decided to try a little flattery. "Of course, you know that, Harold. You don't miss much about your fellow humans."

He smiled. "It's Alice, of course. I have to take her out, and that means I have the opportunity to observe people. And you're right about people wearing funny outfits. A lot of the bodies I see at the beach are showing off far too much skin!"

We both laughed. "It's those beer drinkers I wonder about," I said. "I guess those guys work hard to build those big paunches, so they're determined to show them off. And some women are just as bad!"

"Right. There are a lot of people in bikinis who shouldn't be."

"And hair choler. I mean, color! I can see going frankly fake, but what I hate are these home dye jobs that wind up looking absolutely dead."

"You've got it! I saw a woman with hair that was such a phony black it looked like she'd used shoe polish!"

"Was that the one with the blue shirt and all the jewelry?"

Harold shrugged. "Seems like her shirt was blue, but I wasn't close enough to see her jewelry. She was down at the beach parking lot, getting into a big white van with a bright orange sign on the side."

CHOCOLATE BOOKS

The True History of Chocolate
by Sophie D. Coe and Michael D. Coe
(THAMES & HUDSON)

The Coes' book has just about everything you ever wanted to know about the history of chocolate.

Based on years of research, it starts with pre-Columbian lore and a written history of chocolate and ends with today's attempts to encourage the revival of historic Mayan cacao trees.

This book tells who actually brought chocolate from Spain to France. (Spanish monks apparently sent some as medicine to the Cardinal of Lyon, and he gave a taste to his brother, the fabled Cardinal Richelieu.) It tells how many cacao beans the Aztecs charged for a rabbit. (They used chocolate for money.) It outlines the reasons why in 1675 England's King Charles II tried to outlaw coffeehouses, which also served chocolate. (Hint: These were popular hangouts for men who liked to argue about politics.)

The book also gives a broad overview of chocolate through the ages, describes techniques of processing and serving chocolate in various eras, and recognizes advances in chocolate technology.

Chapter 13

I went straight to the boat shop, of course. I had to share this with Joe.

He immediately tried to share it with Larry Underwood. Underwood, however, wasn't at the Warner Pier PD, and the dispatcher said he wasn't answering his cell phone.

So it was a bit anticlimactic. I stood around the boat shop until my heart quit thumping—though I tried to tell myself I hadn't shown my excitement when Harold dropped the white van with an orange sign on me— then I got in my own van again. And this time I actually went to the grocery store.

The Superette is the only place to buy food in Warner Pier, and its name describes it. It's a minisupermarket. They stock meat, vegetables, bread, and even booze, but it's small. That doesn't mean the selections are limited. It means they're odd. The store caters to summer visitors, so some departments seem skewed. They carry a dozen brands of extra-virgin olive oil, for example, and the cheese counter rivals anything I've seen in Dallas. They have plenty of high-priced steaks—ideal for grilling on the deck of a yacht—but pot roast and stew meat are not always available. Ground round is in greater supply than regular hamburger, and it's easier to find whole-bean coffee than a can of Folgers. Most Warner Pier locals go to a bigger supermarket in Holland to buy staples, but I didn't have time for that.

The biggest drawback to the Superette is its druggist. Greg Glossop is the root and the main stem of the Warner Pier grapevine. I've been known to pluck some information from that grapevine on occasion, so I shouldn't be critical of Mr. Gossip—I mean, Glossop. But on that day I didn't want to see him. I knew he'd be trying to pull information about the holdup out of me, and I wasn't sure what I wanted to tell him.

Sure enough, as soon as I came in the door I saw Glossop in his glass-fronted nest—the pharmacy sits up higher than the rest of the store—and he saw me. His eyes lit up, and he put aside whatever he was working on. A moment later he was out the door of the pharmacy, and we were on a collision course, both aimed for the meat counter.

Faced with a direct confrontation, I decided to attack before Glossop could. Luckily I was able to come up with a harmless topic.

"Mr. Glossop," I said. "What's this I hear about the sale of Warner Pier Wine Shop?"

Glossop's face screwed up. I could see his inner turmoil. He was not as interested in the sale of the wine shop as he was in getting me to talk about the theft of the Double Diamond jewelry, but he did want to know what I'd heard.

He fell for it. "The wine shop? Who bought it?"

"I was hoping you'd know. All the downtown merchants are curious. The word is that it's someone from

Chicago, someone who owns a cottage here." I leaned toward him and dropped my voice. "Have you heard anything?"

"Not a word. Since the VanHulens left town . . ." We both raised our eyebrows. The VanHulens were apparently getting a divorce, and the wine business she'd run seemed to be caught up in the legal proceedings. Everybody in town had already hashed that situation over thoroughly.

"If you hear anything," I said, "I'd sure like to know who our new neighbors are."

Darn. I'd said a word that brought Glossop back to his original purpose.

"Neighbors," he said. "I guess your new neighbors out on the lakeshore gave you an exciting evening." He grinned avidly.

I turned to examine the ground round closely. "The holdup?" I said. "It was a very unpleasant experience."

Glossop was practically drooling. "Just what happened?"

"The police asked me not to discuss it."

"I heard that one of the robbers drowned while trying to swim away."

"I wouldn't know about that." No, the man I'd been asked to identify had supposedly been stabbed, not drowned, but I didn't *know* anything.

Glossop went on. "Everyone's talking about strange cars seen at the beach and—"

"At the beach? That's nothing to get excited about. There are all sorts of strange cars there every day." I gave a smile I hoped looked nervous. "And I've got to rush. I'll see you later."

I grabbed up two packages of ground round and whirled my cart toward the produce aisle. Even Glossop didn't have the nerve to follow me.

But his comment about the strange cars had caught my attention. Surely he hadn't heard about the white van with the orange sign on the door. Of course, if Harold had dropped by for a sack of dog food, it was entirely possible that he'd mentioned the white van to Glossop. The two of them were kindred souls.

If the white van with an orange sign was still around Warner Pier, it ought to be easy to find. White vans were everywhere, true, but this apparently was a commercial van with a painted sign on its door. An orange sign. A vehicle that noticeable wasn't going to be hard to track down. Not that there was a central registry for vehicles entering Warner Pier.

Or was there? I stared at a bunch of broccoli. Maybe there was such a list. As soon as I finished my shopping, I headed for the Warner Pier High School parking lot to check.

In a summer resort like Warner Pier, the population quadruples, maybe even quintuples or octuples, during the months between Memorial Day and Labor Day. Tourists and summer people are drawn to Warner Pier because of our quaint houses and the narrow streets that give the illusion they've returned to the small-town life of the early 1900s. So they all drive into town, and those quaint narrow streets become so clogged that it's almost impossible to drive on them.

In other words, parking is a perpetual problem during the summer in Warner Pier. So the town has come up with several attempts to solve the problem. One of them is that every summer the city leases the school parking lot. High school and college students are hired to staff it, collecting money and allotting slots. Then other students are hired to drive small buses, ferrying drivers the few blocks to the Dock Street Park or to the shops on Peach Street to help them spend their money in Warner Pier.

That summer the head parking lot attendant was Will VanKlompen, Warner Pier High graduate and a sophomore at Michigan State University. Nobody in Warner Pier saw more cars than Will, and he was dating my stepsister, Brenda.

I drove by the parking lot slowly, making sure Will was on duty. As head attendant, Will made up the schedule, and he tended to work the same shifts Brenda worked at the chocolate shop. Funny how that worked out.

Sure enough, Will's big frame was lolling in a lawn chair under a big beach umbrella at the entrance to the parking lot. His hair, sandy in the winter, was now bleached almost white by the sun, and his tan would have given a dermatologist nightmares.

Will wore khaki shorts like all the Warner Pier employers seemed to ask their employees to wear, and the City of Warner Pier's purple-and-gold logo adorned the upper left-hand side of his white polo shirt.

Will was never going to be a handsome guy, but even at nineteen he had a rugged look that was attractive to girls. At the moment he was reading a book and sweating.

I pulled into the drive, stopping beside the wooden A-frame sign that said, LOT FULL in two-foot-high letters.

"Sorry, we're full up," Will hollered first; then he looked up, saw who it was, and came over to my window. "Hi, Lee. What are you up to?"

"I wanted to challenge your observation skills, Will. I'll move on around if somebody needs to come in or go out."

"It's too early for anybody to leave. What did you want me to observe?"

"A white van, commercial type, with an orange sign painted on the door."

"That's an odd combination, but I think there's one here at the moment."

My yell almost deafened Will. "Where?"

"On the back row. It came in this morning. Why did you want to know?"

I didn't answer. "Mind if I take a look at it?"

"It's a public lot." Will came around the van and got in on the passenger side. "I'll soak up a little AC, as long as you're here. Drive around to the right. Why are you interested in this van?"

"I assume Brenda told you Joe's aunt was staying with us?" Will nodded, and I quickly sketched Gina's unexpected and reclusive stay, then sudden departure. I left out the part about the running footprints. But I told him she'd called to say she was all right.

"Anyway," I said, "we can't figure out where she went, and one of the neighbors said he saw a woman with dyed-black hair getting into a big white van with an orange sign on the door."

Will frowned, and I went on. "Now, I know you don't take license numbers or anything. . . ."

"And a lot of tourists don't park in this lot."

"Right. But you still see more cars than nearly anybody else does. So I thought I'd ask. Do you remember who drove this van in?"

Will shook his head. "Sorry. I wasn't on duty. But I doubt anybody remembers who brought it in. The tourists' faces all become a blur."

By then I had reached the back row, and I stopped in front of a blocky white vehicle.

"Did your neighbor say whether it had windows in the back or was enclosed?" Will said.

"No, and I didn't want to ask. What does the sign on the door say?"

We had to get out and walk up next to the van to find out. It was a GMC van, a big one, with windows all around. The sign proved to be a block of orange with white lettering. Frankly, its brightness made it almost impossible to make out.

" 'Orangeman's Electric Service,' " Will read. " 'Residential and Commercial. South Bend.' "

"That's a really odd business name," I said. "At least, if it's located in South Bend, Indiana."

"Why?"

"Because South Bend is the location of Notre Dame University, Will. The Fighting Irish. Anything orange is anathema to them."

Will looked blank. "They don't like orange?"

"Orange is the color of Protestant Ireland. Notre Dame is associated with Catholic Ireland, and its team color is green."

We thoroughly looked the white van over. I noted a couple of scratches, then wrote down the license number. It had an Indiana license plate. When I peeked through the windows, I saw nothing of interest. No papers, no empty cans that had once held exotic brands of beer, no photographs. There wasn't even a beach towel. Not very typical of a vacationer's vehicle.

"I'll be on duty here until eight," Will said. "I'll check on whoever picks it up."

"No!" The memory of the dead man flashed into my mind. "I'll call the state police. They'll know whether or not they need to investigate this vehicle. The owner may be someone completely unconnected with the van our neighbor saw."

He frowned, and I tapped him on the arm. "I'm serious, Will. The people with the van may be dangerous. Or they may be mere tourists. If it's the first, you could endanger yourself if you show too much interest. If it's the second, you could endanger your job for rudeness to visitors!"

Will grinned. "I don't want that to happen," he said. "But if I see any more white vans with orange signs, I'll write their license numbers down."

"Surreptitiously," I said in a stern voice.

"Right. Surreptitiously. Can you lend me a piece of paper?"

On the way home I called Joe and told him about the van. Then I called Underwood. This time the dispatcher tracked the detective down, and in a few minutes he called me back.

I told Underwood what Harold Glick had said and about finding the big white GMC van in the Warner Pier High School parking lot. Underwood didn't act too excited, but he said he'd look into who owned the van in the parking lot.

His reaction was so offhand that I was tempted to do what Will had threatened to do—try to find out who picked up the white van. However, common sense won out, and I started chopping onions for meat loaf.

I did call the shop. Tracy answered the phone, lowered her voice, and told me Dolly was still trying hard to keep chocolate from melting.

"It's not too hot up front in the shop," Tracy said. "I wish we could push some of the cool air back to the workroom—use a fan or something. But Dolly says no."

"I think she's right, Tracy. The chocolate on the shelves in the shop is ready for sale. You can't risk letting it get warm."

I also wanted to know if the girls were coming home to eat. They were. So even with Gina gone, I was still planning on six for dinner, supposing Pete was going to show up.

The answer to that one came at five thirty p.m., when Pete pulled into the drive at almost the same moment Joe and Darrell came in from the boat shop, both completely sweat-soaked. Pete tactfully had brought beer, and the three guys sat on the porch with the box fan blowing on them and drank it. As soon as Brenda and Tracy showed up, I tossed the salad together and told everyone dinner was on the table.

The evening went along routinely, but I was on pins and needles. I wanted to know about that white van in the Warner Pier High School parking lot. I could hardly wait for Will to call.

I'd done the dishes—Joe dried—and Darrell and Pete had announced they were going to go over to the boat shop for showers. That was a smart move.

I was sitting in the living room, with a fan blowing directly on me, when the phone finally rang. I ran for the kitchen and snatched it up.

"Hi, Lee. It's Will."

"Hi. What happened with the van?"

"Nothing! I'm bummed about it."

"What do you mean?"

"I watched it all afternoon. The state cops watched it. But nothing ever happened."

"Nothing?"

"No! The darn thing's still there. Whoever parked it never came back for it. It's a dead end."

Chapter 14

I didn't laugh.

"Will," I said, "what's your major?"

"Electrical engineering. Why?"

"Just wondered." I didn't tell Will it was a good thing he wasn't majoring in law enforcement. He'd never make a detective. "What are the state police doing?"

"They told me to go home."

"Probably a good idea. Unless you and Brenda are going out."

"Maybe down to the Dockster for a while. We won't be late!"

I assured Will I was merely Brenda's landlady, not her chaperone, and I called her to the phone. Then I did laugh. Will, bless his heart, hadn't seen how suspicious the abandonment of the van was. But I thought Underwood had caught on.

I took a cool shower and got ready for bed. Joe came in about ten thirty, but it was too darn hot for either of us to be more than mildly affectionate. I was also aware that I had the noon-to-nine p.m. shift the next day. And if the air-conditioning people hadn't performed miracles during the morning, I'd have to spend an important part of my time hassling them. Hassling them sweetly. I didn't dare make them mad.

I still had the white GMC van—and the air-conditioning—on my mind when I got up at seven thirty the next morning. Pete was already gone, but he had made coffee and left a cereal bowl in the sink. The girls were still asleep, Joe was beginning to move around, and Darrell hadn't come in. My brain was barely percolating.

Then Underwood's unmarked car parked in the drive.

I called out the dining room window, "Hi! I hear the white van was never claimed last night."

Underwood nodded.

"Did anybody pick it up after the lot closed?"

He shook his head.

"Come on in. The coffee's made."

Underwood shook his head again. Odd that he wasn't saying anything. And he wasn't coming to the house either. He had another detective with him, and they were walking toward Darrell's camper.

I watched as they stood on either side of the door; then the second detective rapped sharply on the aluminum. "Open up! Police!"

I ran for the bedroom. "Joe! Underwood's arresting Darrell!"

"Huh?" Joe's voice came from the bathroom behind me. He opened the door, holding his toothbrush and with foam on his lips.

"Hurry! Underwood and another detective are banging on Darrell's door. I think they're arresting him!"

"Surely not." Joe sounded calm.

I ran through the kitchen, then out onto the back

porch. Darrell was standing in the door of his camper, wearing boxers and looking bleary-eyed. "Sure," he said. "I don't mind talking to you. Mind if I get some clothes on?"

Before Darrell came out again, Joe was going toward the back door. I was still feeling panicky, but he patted my hand. "Don't say anything," he said. "It looks like it's just routine. They must have found out that Darrell was once charged with home invasion."

"But he was exonerated!"

"No, Lee. He was exonerated on a murder charge. He never denied he and a buddy had entered a drug dealer's home at gunpoint. We were able to prove—finally—that the drug dealer was still alive when they left. Darrell was never prosecuted for the home invasion, but he was charged."

He smiled reassuringly. "Don't worry yet. I still think it's probably routine."

So I stood on the porch like the little woman while Joe walked out—barefoot—and talked to Underwood in a low voice for a few minutes. Then he gestured toward the house and spoke a little more loudly. "Do you want to come in?"

Underwood grinned. "Darrell would probably like the PD better. It's air conditioned. I see you've got all your windows open." Joe and both detectives laughed, not very humorously.

But they did come in the house. Darrell, Joe, and the two detectives sat around the dining table. Joe turned on the fan, and everyone accepted a cup of coffee. Which cleaned out the pot, so I started a new one, then went into the bedroom to get dressed. When I came back into the kitchen—Joe obviously didn't want me to join the group, but I could eavesdrop from the next room—things were still sounding friendly.

"So you were here all evening," Underwood was saying. "Joe and Lee were at the Garretts' house, of course. Can anyone else substantiate your actions?"

"Sure," Darrell said. "Pete was here. And Ms. Woodyard—Joe's aunt."

"She's missing."

"Yeah, but when she turns up, she'll tell you. I was here all evening."

Joe spoke. "What about Brenda and Tracy?"

"They went out for a while," Darrell said. "Those two guys they date came for them. I didn't pay any attention to where they said they were going."

"Probably cruising up and down Peach Street," Joe said.

Underwood went on. "But Pete Falconer can back your story up?"

"Well, for most of the evening he can. We watched the baseball game. But he went out for a while. He said he was going to get some beer."

"How long was he gone?"

"Half an hour. Maybe forty-five minutes. I didn't check."

"Was Gina Woodyard watching the game with you?"

"No. She went upstairs. Said she was going to read a book."

"So there were forty-five minutes when you were alone?"

"Alone in the living room. But Ms. Woodyard was upstairs. She would have heard me if I'd gone anyplace."

Underwood turned to Joe. "Did she have a fan upstairs? A fan's pretty noisy."

"The one she has is fairly quiet. And Gina doesn't miss much."

"When we find her," Underwood said, "we'll ask if she heard anybody leave. Anybody but Falconer."

When Underwood went on, his voice was almost too casual. "Darrell, do you mind if we take a look inside the camper?"

I was pleased to hear Darrell answer without hesitation. "Be my guest. It's full of dirty clothes."

"We can stand it."

The two detectives went out to the camper. I brought the cereal and milk into the dining room. Joe, Darrell, and I might as well go through the motions of having breakfast.

"Thank goodness the girls are sleeping through all this," I said. "Tracy would have a routine episode made into a novel by lunchtime."

Neither Joe nor Darrell laughed. But each of them did pour a bowl of cereal, and Joe calmly spoke to Darrell, telling him he'd handled the questions exactly the right way.

Darrell frowned. "I'll feel better once Pete and Ms. Woodyard have backed me up," he said.

We could see Underwood and his fellow detective out at the camper. They weren't tearing the mattress apart, but they weren't simply looking around either. Darrell was going to have some straightening up to do after they left.

I was still eating cornflakes when they brought a mesh bag out the camper's back door. "I guess they really are going to check your dirty clothes," I said.

Darrell growled. "Serves 'em right. I've been sweating like a pig."

We all smiled a little, but we each kept an eye on the two searchers. So we all three knew exactly the moment when they found something.

None of us said anything. We simply watched as Underwood and his assistant turned their backs toward us, threw their shoulders together, and formed a wall—a wall that hid some object from us. Their ducked heads told us they were examining it closely. Underwood kept that posture, using his body to hide whatever he'd found, while his helper went to the car and came back with a sheaf of papers.

"They've found something they find interesting, Darrell," Joe said calmly. "Can you think what it might be?"

"Not drugs! Joe, I'm absolutely clean. There's nothing in that camper that shouldn't be there."

"I believe you."

For a few minutes I thought Underwood and the other detective were going to drive away without asking Darrell about what they'd found, or even telling him what it was. But after they'd pawed through the rest of the dirty clothes, they came to the back door. Underwood was polite enough to knock on the screen door.

Joe told them to come on in. "What did you find?" he said. He made the question sound unimportant.

Underwood came into the dining room and laid the paper bag on the table.

"We found this wrapped in a T-shirt," he told Darrell. "What do you know about it?" He gently nudged the brown bag until the object inside slid out.

It was a crescent moon, about an inch and a half from tip to tip. It was gold, set with pearls, and a strong-looking metal clasp stretched across its back.

"I never saw it before," Darrell said.

Underwood held up the papers his assistant had brought from the car. " 'Fifteen-carat gold new-moon pin, set with split pearls,' " he read. " 'Circa 1900. Valued at two to three hundred dollars.' " He dropped the papers and looked at Darrell. "It's on the inventory of the stolen jewelry."

Darrell dropped his head, looking completely beaten. "I don't know how it got there," he said dully.

I guess it was his defeated look that made me mad.
"No!" I jumped to my feet and yelled out the word.
"If y'all are trying to say Darrell was one of the robbers who held us up at the Garretts' house, y'all are
flat crazy!"

"Mrs. Woodyard—" Underwood didn't sound
apologetic.

"Don't you 'Mrs. Woodyard' me!" I said. "When
you were drinking my coffee and acting friendly I
was Lee."

"I appreciate your loyalty to a guest—" Underwood said.

I didn't let him finish whatever he was about to say.
"Loyalty, my foot! I'm not loyal. I'm observant. I saw
those three robbers! They pointed pistols at me! One
was taller than Darrell. One was shorter and fatter.
And one had an onion—I mean, a bunion! He had a
bunion on his right foot!" I thumped the table. "None
of them was daring! I mean Darrell. Darrell was not
one of them!"

Darrell had raised his head and dropped his jaw,
looking astonished. Underwood and his assistant had
put on their detective faces—strictly unemotional. It
was Joe who laughed.

Then he got up and gave me a kiss on the cheek.
"Lee, the state police don't want to arrest the wrong
guy. But you can see they're going to have to ask
some questions about that pin."

He slid his arm around my shoulders. "So if they
take Darrell in for questioning, my job will be to go
along for moral support. Your job will be to make a
list of everybody who was in the neighborhood yesterday. Everybody who would have had a chance to plant
that pin in Darrell's dirty clothes."

When he went on, I knew he wasn't really talking
to me. "Because you are completely right," he said.

"We both know Darrell had nothing to do with that holdup."

I shut up after that. Joe, after all, had been a defense attorney. I could count on him to handle it. So I stood by while the detectives sealed up Darrell's camper, then escorted him to their car. I was doing fine until Darrell started to get into the backseat. I was watching from the dining room window, and he turned and yelled at me, "Thanks, Lee!"

I went into the bedroom and burst into tears. Joe was in there, hastily putting on khakis and a knit shirt, and my crying jag scared him into next week.

I found it hard to explain. "Darrell's just had so many bad knocks. He ought to be raging mad, not thanking me for my pitiful efforts to stand up for him. Which probably made things worse."

"I doubt that you made things worse. Underwood's not a bully, but it won't hurt for him to know Darrell has friends."

"I'm sure Darrell wasn't involved in that robbery. But I wish I could do something to help him."

"You can. I already told you we need to check and see who was around yesterday."

"We need to find Gina, too. I'm terribly worried about her." I gasped. "I forgot! If that van was abandoned in the high school parking lot, it's probably been impounded."

"At least Underwood will know who it's registered to," Joe said. "I'll try to find an opportunity to ask him. You canvass the neighbors. Find out who was around the neighborhood yesterday, even if it was only the UPS man. And try to find Pete. If he can back up Darrell's story, it will be a major help."

"How would I know where to find Pete? He's in a tree someplace, right? Peeping at some bird."

"Yes, but he should have his phone, even if it's set on vibrate."

I said good-bye to Joe as he left, and then yelled up the stairs to tell the girls I needed to talk to them. I called Pete's cell phone number and left a message on his voice mail. I hoped that the vibration tickled his tummy, but the lakeshore is a notoriously bad location for cell phone reception, so I wasn't very optimistic. I also wrote a note with a bright red marker and pinned it to the kitchen door. If Pete came back to the house, he'd surely find it.

I contemplated knocking on the neighbors' doors and decided I'd better look halfway decent before I took on that job. I tried to put on a little makeup—not easy when sweat is washing it off faster than you can rub it on. I brushed my hair into a ponytail and hoped I didn't look like a madwoman. Which was what I felt like.

But in half an hour I was reasonably presentable and had brought Brenda and Tracy up-to-date on what had happened with Darrell. I was pleased that they didn't immediately assume his guilt. Neither of them was friendly with Darrell—and I guess I hadn't felt too friendly toward him either before I heard more about his background—so I hadn't known what their reactions would be.

Then I got a pad and pencil and started plodding around the neighborhood. I wasn't going to do it fast. The temperature was rising rapidly, right in tandem with the humidity. I thought longingly of Prairie Creek, Texas, and how dry the heat was there. And how well my dad's air-conditioning worked.

My stop at Harold's was a replay of the stop I'd made there twenty-four hours earlier, when he told me about seeing Gina get into the white van. Once again Alice ran out to greet me. Once again Harold came out onto the porch. Once again I could hear his blessed air-conditioning humming. Once again he didn't invite me inside.

I just told him that some prowler had apparently gotten into Darrell's camper, and that we were trying to figure out who it was.

"You get around the neighborhood more than most," I said. "Did you see anybody wandering around yesterday?"

"Anybody strange?"

"No. Anybody at all. Even, you know, the UPS man or the meter reader."

Harold looked amazed. "You think someone like that might have fooled around with that old camper?"

"No, no! But they might have seen someone doing it."

"Oh! I get it." Harold enumerated several possibilities. I didn't find any of them too startling. Not only had the UPS man come by, but FedEx had made deliveries, too. The mailman had come, of course. Harold hadn't seen a meter reader of any type, but the cable service truck had been parked on Lake Shore Drive. Someone on the lake side had had a tree removal firm working. And Wednesday was the regular day for Lakeside Lawn Service to hit its clients in the neighborhood.

"I don't know if that helps," Harold said.

"I don't know either," I said. "But thanks."

I scratched Alice under the chin and walked on. I visited half a dozen houses where people were home, and a dozen where no one answered. I left notes at those.

One of the apparently empty houses was the Garretts'. When I walked up the drive I thought I saw a curtain twitch, but no one came to the door, so I decided it was merely blowing in the breeze. Not that there was a lot of breeze. I could barely breathe. I left a note for Alex Gold.

It was after eleven when I got home, walking even more slowly than I had when I started out. The heat and humidity had melted me into a pool of exhausted sweat. And now it was time for me to work an eight-hour shift. I decided to eat lunch in town—someplace air conditioned.

So I was in the Sidewalk Café, drinking genuine brewed iced tea, when my cell phone rang. I was glad to see Joe's name appear on the screen.

I didn't even say hello. "What's going on?"

"I guess they're going to hold Darrell until Pete shows up. But that's not why I'm calling."

"Now what's happened?"

"Underwood finally told me who that white GMC van that was abandoned is registered to." He took a deep breath. "Lee, it was registered in Indiana, but it belongs to Art Atkins."

"Gina's husband?"

"Right. Do you think there's any possibility that she went off with him willingly?"

"No!" I said. "He's dead."

Chapter 15

Joe replied like a true lawyer—cautiously. "Lee, we aren't sure that the dead man is Art Atkins."

"I know, but it sure looks likely. And in any case, I can't imagine that Gina would have gone off with her ex. She'd been avoiding him for ten days."

"She was avoiding someone, Lee. We don't know that it was Art Atkins. It could have been someone else. Heck, she may owe somebody money."

I thought about it. "True. But debt collectors don't usually inspire terror. Just dread. Has Underwood been able to find out anything about Atkins?"

"He doesn't have a criminal record. I guess that's some comfort, but it's not real helpful."

"Underwood doesn't know what he looks like?"

"Atkins doesn't have a Michigan driver's license, so Underwood hasn't located a picture of him. I'm going to call Grandma Ida and see if she has one."

"Oh, gee! I hate to get Grandma Ida involved. But I'm really getting worried about Gina." I gasped. "Joe, I was forgetting. Right before Gina ran off, she called those Holland motels and asked for him."

"But she asked for Andy Woodyard, too."

"Did Underwood check to see if anybody using either name was registered in Holland?"

"If he did, he didn't tell me. I'll ask and call you back. You haven't heard from Pete, have you?"

I told Joe about the phone calls and messages I'd left for Pete.

"I sure wish I knew where to find him," he said. "I think they'd let Darrell go if Pete backed him up. I'll talk to you later."

I hung up and paid my check. But my mind was on Pete. Darrell needed to find him right away. But where could Pete be? He'd left a note saying he was going bird-watching. Birds were not exactly rare along the lakeshore, and Pete could be looking at them anywhere. He'd never given a hint as to where his main bird-watching hangouts were.

Or had he?

When he'd shown us the picture of the owl that caught the rabbit, the owl had been taking off from a red tile roof.

Red tiles. *Hmmm.*

If I were back in Texas, red tiles would have been fairly easy to find. We have plenty of Spanish-style architecture in the Lone Star State.

But along the shore of Lake Michigan, the architecture tends toward Victorian, Craftsman, or even modern. None of those styles normally uses red-tiled roofs. But there was one place: the River Villa. And it would be an ideal spot for bird-watching.

The River Villa was built around 1910 by some Chicago millionaire who apparently had spent too much time on the Mediterranean. He created a fantasy Italian villa with stucco walls and a red tile roof. Little balconies and turrets were tacked on here and there with no apparent attention to the overall plan.

Originally, or so the local historians say, the River

Villa employed a staff of twenty-five. Its original owner—or his wife—was a patron of the arts, and throughout the 1920s they kept an open house for Warner Pier's art colony and for their Jazz Age friends from Chicago. The Depression of the 1930s ended that life. The River Villa was abandoned, its balconies falling down, its patios and flower beds gradually plowed up by maples.

The house sat on a thousand acres that Warner Pier of the 1920s and 1930s had called worthless. It was worthless in those days because it wasn't suitable for fruit trees, then the main cash crop of the area, and later it was considered worthless for building vacation cottages, because it was too far up the Warner River. Prime building lots then were on the lake, and there was still lots of lakefront property in those days.

Today the property would be valuable for development as home sites. Unfortunately, the heirs couldn't decide what to do with the place, so it just sat there. The house had been considered for a bed-and-breakfast, for a resort, for a school. But the heirs couldn't agree on who should buy or lease. It was rented to two artists, and they held classes in what was once the ballroom. The grounds were completely overgrown.

So the place had a red tile roof, and it ought to have lots of birds. Maybe it was where Pete had been watching owls. It was possible to drive into the grounds, and I decided it might be worth doing that, just to see if Pete's forest green SUV was parked anywhere obvious.

I called the shop to say I'd be late. I didn't have the nerve to talk to Dolly Jolly. I'd ignored her and her problems all day, and my conscience was eating at me. Luckily, Tracy answered the phone and told me the air-conditioning crew was there, so that made me feel a little better as I got into my red van and drove off in the wrong direction, away from my duty to chocolate.

The River Villa had a gravel parking lot near the house, and a meandering dirt road looped through the site. Pete's SUV was not in the main parking lot, so I started along the drive. I drove slowly, partly because the road was full of potholes.

I had swung around the property and was headed back to the main gate when I saw a glint down a road that looked as if it might lead to a garbage pit. And there, behind a bush, was a forest green SUV, its color camouflaging it from casual glances.

I stopped the van and walked over to the SUV. A peek through the front window and I was sure. Pete's wide-brimmed bush hat was in the front seat. I'd found his ride.

But where was Pete? I looked all around. No sign of him.

Why had he parked in this hidden spot? The River Villa renters didn't seem to be concerned about trespassers. If Pete wanted to walk around the property and look at birds, why not park in the official parking area?

There were two obvious answers. The first was, Pete didn't want someone to know he was there. The second was, he was looking at something close to this particular spot, and he wanted to be able to get back to his car in a hurry.

I went back to my van, found a pad and pencil in my purse, and wrote a note telling Pete he was needed quickly at the Warner Pier PD. *Bring Darrell an alibi for Saturday night,* I wrote. I walked back to his SUV and stuck the note under a windshield wiper.

Then I took another look around. I couldn't believe Pete wasn't close by. I called his name: "Pete!" But somehow I didn't want to yell it out loudly.

I was turning to leave when I saw a path. It didn't look exactly well traveled, but it led downhill, toward the river. I hesitated only a moment before I followed it.

I was immediately sorry. Mosquitoes and deer flies the size of pigeons descended. All I had for protective gear was a chocolate brown polo shirt and a pair of khaki slacks. I pulled the neckline of the shirt up over my head, pretending it was a hood. This left a strip of my back in peril. I almost turned around. But then I saw a footprint that looked a lot like it might be Pete's, and I couldn't resist going on.

After running the gauntlet of mosquitoes and flies through thick woods for about fifty feet, I came to an area where the trees abruptly cleared. I left the woods and found myself on the bank of the Warner River. Actually, I nearly found myself *in* the river. The last few feet were steep, and I slid down the path rather dramatically, giving a loud yelp as my feet went out from under me and I sat down harder than I really like to sit. When I stopped sliding my feet were just a foot from the water.

The path continued upstream. I stood up, taking in my surroundings.

And the first surrounding I noticed was two guys in a boat, laughing at me.

One of them, a plump type, hollered, "You okay?"

I waved feebly. "Just surprised!"

I walked along the path, trying not to stare at the boat, but it had surprised me as much as my sudden slide had. It surprised me because it was so close.

The town of Warner Pier was built where the river deepens before it enters the lake, at a spot where it is possible to load cargo boats. Upstream the river tends to become wide and swampy. But at this spot it was narrower and deeper than I'd expected. So the two men in the boat were only fifty feet or so away.

They were tying up a very ordinary fiberglass boat at a ramshackle dock. Joe, the expert on antique wooden boats, would have sneered at theirs. The cottage behind it was a real fixer-upper, and a very ordinary blue pickup sat beside it.

I had no idea anything as tumbledown as that cottage remained on the Warner River. Property values for anything with a view of the water—whether lake or river—had gone through the roof; if people couldn't afford to keep their property up, they sold it and lived off the proceeds.

But I didn't pay a lot of attention to the men, their boat, or the cottage behind them. I simply walked on up the path along the river, looking into the woods for a glimpse of Pete. After a hundred feet or so I hadn't seen him, and the bugs were still bombarding me, so I turned around and started back.

From this direction I could see the two men with the boat without turning my head, so I took a good look at them. Somehow they seemed familiar. One was tall, and the other was short. Then I saw them eyeing me the way I was eyeing them, and I quickly began to examine the woods again. I refrained from calling out Pete's name, however.

A tall guy and a short guy. Lofty and Shorty. The same combination as the two men who had held us at gunpoint.

Then I told myself I was seeing bad guys everywhere, and I kept walking.

Finding where the path started up the bank didn't prove to be too easy, but I spotted it. I slipped and slid up the slope, whacking at insects like a windmill, keeping my head down to make sure I didn't fall again and this time sprain an ankle.

I was still looking at the ground when I reached the road, and a voice growled. "Just what the hell do you think you're doing?"

After I'd jumped as high as the trees that arched over us, I realized that Pete, the missing bird-watcher himself, was leaning against his SUV. His binoculars were hanging around his neck, and he was scowling like an eagle who's just lost a rotten fish to a loon. And I was the loon.

"Pete! You didn't have to scare the sacks—I mean, the socks! You didn't have to startle me like that!"

"I wish I could scare you! How did you know where to find me?"

"Just a guess. That picture of an owl you showed us included a red roof, so I figured the River Villa was one place you'd been looking at birds. When I saw your SUV . . ."

"You just naturally went down to the river and nearly fell in."

"You saw me? Why didn't you say something?" I was getting mad.

"What's to say? What are you doing here?"

I stabbed my forefinger toward his windshield. "An emergency came up. Joe needs to find you. You didn't answer your phone."

Pete snatched the note from the windshield. "And you leave information just lying around where anybody in the world could find it!"

"Look! If you want to communicate with us by cider—I mean, by cipher! If you want secret messages, you're going to have to give me a codebook. Good-bye!"

I shoved past Pete and headed for my van, but he grabbed my arm. He swung me around. His binoculars were digging into my chest. Suddenly we were nose-to-nose again, just as we had been under the tarp a day earlier. And the same thing happened. We stood there staring at each other.

I shoved Pete's hand off my arm. "I'm leaving," I said. "I'm late getting to the office because I was trying to find you. Joe and I would appreciate it if you'd go by the Warner Pier PD and tell the cops whether or not you can say where Darrell was during that robbery at the Garretts'."

I guess I had the last word. Anyway, Pete didn't answer me. I got into the van and drove away.

Pete was the most arrogant jerk I'd ever been around. And what the heck was he up to out at the River Villa? He definitely was not watching birds.

I hadn't been at my desk long when Joe called. "Hey, Lee," he said. "Underwood found out that an Andrew Woodyard had been registered at the Holiday Inn Express in Holland for the past week. He checked out Wednesday."

I had to pull my mind back to what Joe and I had been talking about an hour earlier. "The motels? The ones Gina called? Andrew Woodyard? Someone was using your dad's name? That's spooky."

"I know. Underwood's sending one of his men over there with a picture of the dead man."

"But we already know the dead man was claiming to be Andrew Woodyard! What we don't know is who he really was."

"Yeah. And getting the motel to ID him isn't going to get closer to that."

I told Joe I'd found Pete, but I didn't tell him the circumstances. Then I tried to work the rest of my shift. Joe called at six o'clock to say that Pete had shown up to alibi Darrell, and the state police were letting Darrell go. The three of them were going out to dinner, he said. He invited me to join them, but his invitation didn't sound real enthusiastic. I told him I'd eat at my desk. Brenda went down to the corner for sandwiches for herself, Tracy, and me, and the three of us—the entire staff of TenHuis Chocolade after five thirty—concentrated on getting everything done so we could leave early. Not that it worked. The tourists kept coming in to suck up our air-conditioning until the moment I locked the door at nine p.m.

Brenda, Tracy, and I celebrated with chocolate. My Crème de Menthe Bonbon ("the formal after-dinner mint") had a bit of bloom, but I found it reviving. Then we got busy, and we finished with the cleanup and money balancing by nine twenty. The boyfriends were going to some guy thing that night, so Brenda and Tracy were free, but they decided to stop by some teenage hangout on the way home. I told the girls I'd see them later and drove home, dreading the stag party I'd find there.

But the house was dark. It stays light until nearly ten o'clock in our part of Michigan in July. If Pete, Joe, and Darrell had come in since dinner, it had still been light when they left again. In fact, I felt sure they hadn't come in; Joe would have left the porch light on for me.

I was so tired that I forgot where I'd been putting my car. I had parked in my own driveway before I remembered Joe and I had been leaving our cars at the Baileys' house.

I was too tired to care. I decided somebody else could park at the Baileys' that night. I got out of the car, slammed the door hard, and tromped to the back door. I unlocked it, went inside, and turned on the kitchen and dining room lights. The dining room light shone into the living room, and I could see there was no mail on the mantel, the designated spot for it. That meant that no one had even walked down to the road and picked it up. I wasn't going to do it either, I decided. I threw my purse down on the dining table in disgust, then kicked off the rubber-soled loafers I usually wear to the office.

If I was alone in the house at least I could use the bathroom without wondering if someone was pacing back and forth outside the door. Barefoot, I started to that room by way of the back hall.

But I never made it. I'd barely entered the back hall when someone knocked on the front door.

The knock only added to my annoyance. Who the heck could that be? With my luck it would be Harold and his darn dog, Alice, dropping by to pass on some useless information.

That back hall had four doors off it. The one I'd just passed through led to the kitchen. The one to its left, always kept closed, led to the basement. The one on the right led to the bathroom. The one in front of me led into the downstairs bedroom—the bedroom I shared with Joe. And a door at the other end of that room led to the living room and the front door.

Still angry, I veered toward the bedroom, the most direct route to the front door.

When I entered the bedroom, all the curtains and the windows were open. Since there are lots of windows in that room, I could see out on the south side, which overlooks the front porch, and on the west side, which overlooks the side yard.

I wasn't surprised to see a dark figure on the porch. Someone had just knocked on the front door, after all.

But I was surprised to see a second dark figure going past the windows on the west.

Someone was walking through the side yard. It was someone tall. What was he doing there?

I looked back at the porch. The man out there was short.

A short guy and a tall guy. The two robbers in the wet suits. And the two guys in the boat, the ones who had laughed when I slid down the bank.

And Pete had been "watching birds" in their vicinity.

I realized the guys in the boat must have been the same guys who had been in the snapshots Pete had shown me. The guys whom he had photographed at Beech Tree Public Access Area.

A tall guy and a short guy. Lofty and Shorty.

The fellow on the front porch knocked again.

He could knock all night, I decided. There was no way I was opening that door.

Chapter 16

Our old house was easy to break into. Even when it was locked up, anybody with a rock could get in through one of our casement windows. Plus, at that moment the back door and all the downstairs windows were standing wide open because of the heat wave.

And some guy I thought was a crook was knocking at the one locked door, and a man I assumed was his pal was heading around the house.

What was I going to do?

I could run out the back.

No, that wouldn't work. The tall guy was obviously getting in position to cut off my escape that way.

I could run upstairs.

That wouldn't do a lot of good either. There was a phone there, true, but I'd have to go through the living room to get to the stairs, and I'd turned on the dining room light, so the living room wasn't dark. Again, all the curtains and blinds were open. If I went into the living room, one of the guys outside—either the tall one at the back of the house or the short one on the porch—would see me go. They'd know I was trapped up there.

I could climb out the bedroom window.

No, the windows were open, but I'd have to push the screen off. I knew from experience that those screens needed a good noisy bang before they came out of the frame. The bad guys would hear that and be outside to meet me.

I couldn't go out the front, out the back, out the side, or upstairs.

I had to go down.

I edged into the back hall. The kitchen light crossed only one corner of it, and I was able to slip around and get to the door that led to the basement.

The basement might turn out to be as much a trap as the upstairs could be—maybe more. Upstairs I at least could climb out onto the roof and start yelling. But I thought I could sneak into the basement without being seen.

I opened the basement door. Joe had recently gone through the house and oiled all the hinges, so it didn't make a sound. I stepped onto the top step and silently closed the door behind myself.

It was dark.

The old TenHuis house has a feature common in houses built around the turn of the twentieth century in our part of the country: a Michigan basement.

I've never been able to discover why a Michigan basement is named for our state. Surely they are found in Minnesota, Indiana, and Wisconsin, too. Are they known as Michigan basements in other states? Or does the owner of a house with a similar feature outside South Bend describe it as "an Indiana basement"?

A Michigan basement has stone or concrete walls, but a sand floor. It's a far cry from a suburban basement with a paneled recreation room. It's more like a root cellar. In Texas we have storm cellars, and the old-fashioned ones are a lot like Michigan basements, except that they're found outdoors, not under the house.

A Michigan basement may be the scariest place in the world. Aunt Nettie is reasonably neat, but a Michigan basement is used only for storage of nonperishable items and as a haven for spiders and, probably, for mice. Nothing in the world short of two bad guys breaking in upstairs would have forced me down there barefoot, in the dark, with no flashlight.

By then I was hearing footsteps in the house. Then quiet voices. The intruders didn't know that there were no secrets in that house. Every movement, every word spoken could be heard upstairs and down. Even in the basement.

The back door guy had apparently let the front door guy in. Their voices came from the living room.

"Where'd she go?"

"I'll look in the bedroom."

"She's probably in the bathroom."

"Without a light?"

Very shortly one of them was going to go into that back hall and open all four doors that led off of it. And I was frozen halfway down the basement steps. When the door above me opened, I'd be in plain view.

I moved down another step, and as I groped along, my hand closed around a pole. I realized it was the handle of the mop, which should have been in the kitchen closet. Brenda had mopped the kitchen two nights earlier, and she'd left the mop on the stairs to dry. At the time I'd been annoyed. That wasn't a good place for a mop, but I never got around to moving it to the right place. Now I gripped it—not as a weapon, but maybe as a distraction.

In another common architectural practice, the stairs to the second floor of our house are directly above the stairs to the basement. The two sets of steps run parallel, one on top of the other.

I grabbed hold of that mop and turned it around, sponge side up. Then I held it up over my head and aimed it at the ceiling over the door I'd come in. That would be the location of the bottom side of one of the steps that led to the second floor. I hoped.

Gently I bumped the bottom of the step. It made a small sound.

I wanted the two intruders to think I was sneaking up the stairs.

Immediately, I heard steps going into the living room. "She's going upstairs!" The guys weren't even trying to be quiet now. They began thumping up the stairs over my head.

Still clutching the mop, I slid my bare foot down another step. Now that my eyes were adjusted to the darkness, I could see a bit from the faint light coming in around the door. And I knew where there was a box of matches in that basement. All I had to do was find it without stepping on something sharp or cracking my head on a rafter. Or making noise by knocking something over.

I carefully felt for the next step down, then for another. But I had to hurry. The tall guy and the short guy wouldn't take long to figure out that I wasn't upstairs. Then they'd start on the downstairs again, and the basement wouldn't be far behind.

It seemed an eternity before I stepped onto sand, and I knew I'd reached the bottom. I turned sharply right and put one hand out in front of me. I walked straight ahead until my hand came in contact with bricks. I'd come up against the base of the chimney.

Now, looking to my right, I could see a blue flicker. The hot-water tank sat on a special little square of concrete, and light from the burner was leaking out underneath it. I knew that on top of that hot-water tank there was a box of matches.

All I had to do to get access to light was reach the hot-water tank without falling over a box of old dishes or some other item my ancestors had deemed too valuable to throw out but not valuable enough to keep upstairs. And these stored items were all hard, too. Nobody would store old curtains or cotton batting down there with the mice and spiders. No, the boxes held things that would make a loud noise if they were knocked over.

Miraculously, I didn't fall over any of them getting to the hot-water tank. I picked up the box of matches. It didn't feel exactly full. But I could hear the tall guy and the short guy thumping around, so I had to keep moving. I stood the mop up against the wall, pulled a match out, and struck it on the side of the box.

As the match flared, I looked behind the hot-water tank.

Thank God. I'd remembered right. The hole in the foundation, covered with a sheet of plywood, was large enough for me to crawl through.

The hole started about three feet off the basement floor and was part of our renovation project. It led to the area Joe and Darrell had dug out for the addition to the bathroom and kitchen. The addition would not have a basement, but needed a deep area for plumbing. Eventually the hole would link that area to the basement itself, where the furnace and hot-water heater were. The plywood was a halfhearted effort at keeping chipmunks and other critters outside while the building project was going on.

Now, if Joe and Darrell just hadn't screwed the plywood in . . . I shoved on the plywood. It gave easily. Apparently they'd simply leaned it up against the wall from the other side.

It wasn't the easiest thing I ever did, but I managed to push the plywood far enough aside to get my fingers around it, and then to lay it flat. Climbing into the hole was faster. The hardest part was putting the plywood back up so that my escape hatch wouldn't be obvious to the bad guys when they explored the basement.

I'm sure I made noise. But by now the intruders were thundering through the house, making so much noise of their own that I didn't worry about it.

The next part of the process was to crawl out into the yard, which was a snap, since the subfloor for the bathroom addition wasn't in yet. The bad guys had turned on every light in the house as they searched for me, so light was flooding out the windows and illuminating the yard.

In only a few seconds I was outside, standing with my back to the wall of the house. That wasn't a safe spot. After they were sure I wasn't inside, the two searchers would start looking outside. I paused a moment, deciding which way to run.

And I heard one of the guys say, "I'm going to bust Haney with an antique baseball bat over this. It was a waste of time from the beginning."

"But she saw us."

"So what? She can't ID us. We should have let it go."

I guess *go* was the word I'd been waiting for. I didn't wait to hear more. I took off for the sandy lane that led to Lake Shore Drive. I ran through the beach grass in our yard—not exactly a lawn—and when I got to the sand I turned toward Lake Shore Drive. I wasn't sure where I was headed, but I knew I wanted to be where there were people—people I could trust.

I kept running, but I sure would have liked to have had a pair of shoes.

I barely paused when I got to the road. Which way? Who would be home? And could I trust them? Those were two important questions.

Ahead of me I saw a light through the trees. It was coming from Double Diamond.

The Double Diamond driveway was dark and twisty, but if a light was on, it probably meant there was someone at the house. Even if it were only Garnet's uncle Alex, he ought to have a phone with 911 on its number pad, and I could be pretty sure he wasn't in with the thieves. After all, they'd robbed *him*.

I ran across the road—it's amazing how much gravel travels onto a blacktop road from the shoulder—and started down the drive. I was fervently wishing for the flashlight Joe and I had used on Saturday night. Then I realized I was still holding the box of matches.

They weren't a lot of help, since they dazzled my eyes, but they gave me moral courage, I guess. I stumbled on, lighting one only when desperate, until I came to the flagstone walk that led to the bungalow's porch. I yelled. "Help! Mr. Gold! It's Lee Woodyard!"

I made my way toward the porch, calling out again every few steps. I was conscious of movement behind the living room windows, and before I got to the door the porch light came on. Then the door opened. Alex Gold stood in the door.

"Mrs. Woodyard?"

"Phone! I need to call the police!"

He was still standing in the door, but I shoved him aside and stumbled into the cottage, blurting out my story of intruders in the house.

I will say Uncle Alex reacted quickly, dashing to a phone on a desk in the corner of the living room. He called 911, and I sank into a chair and massaged my feet.

I groaned. My grandmother told me that as a child in Texas she went barefoot until her feet were one big callus. She swore she could walk on gravel and not flinch. Right at that moment I would have given anything to have feet that tough. Alex Gold was wearing a neat pair of house slippers, and I could see a pair of rubber flip-flops near the front door. I lusted after both pairs of shoes.

Uncle Alex was talking to the 911 operator. "Yes, we'll hold the line until they come. Do you want to talk to Mrs. Woodyard?" He listened; then held the phone out toward me. "The dispatcher has sent a car, but she wants to make sure there is no one in the house but the intruders."

The girls!

The knowledge hit me like a knife in the back. Brenda and Tracy had planned to come home as soon as they cruised by someplace for a Coke. They might be pulling into our drive any minute.

"Oh, no!" I jumped to my feet. "The girls were coming home right away! The bad guys might still be there! I have to stop them!"

I didn't ask permission to borrow Alex's flip-flops. I simply jammed my feet into them and ran out the front door.

I stumbled my way back down that dark drive. I was terrified. I might be only their landlady, not their chaperone, but the thought of those girls driving up and surprising the two robbers . . .

The prospect of having to tell my stepmother and Tracy's parents that their daughters had been shot dead turned me into an Olympic runner.

At least, I suppose I ran. I don't remember how I got down that drive. I may have swum, crawled, or done cartwheels. I just knew I had to head Brenda and Tracy off. I could not let them drive up to the house and meet those two bad guys.

Just as I got to Lake Shore Drive, the lights of a car appeared to my right, coming toward me. Brenda and Tracy should be coming from the left. I was already panicky, and that car raised my panic to red-flag levels. Who was it? By now the bad guys must know I'd escaped from the house. They might be cruising the neighborhood looking for me.

I jumped behind a bush. I did not want to take a chance on any strangers at that point. No, I'd lie low until the car was past, and I could run across and hide in the undergrowth beside our drive, ready to jump out and wave Brenda's car down.

To my horror the car slowed, and I realized it was turning into our drive. Then I heard the music coming from the vehicle. There could only be one car in western Michigan that played country music every moment the motor was running. I might not be able to see the color, but I knew that was Brenda's car.

I plunged across the road and into the headlights, waving. Brenda's brakes screeched. Luckily she was able to stop.

I ran up to the passenger's side and grabbed the door handle. "Quick! Let me in! Get out of here!" I yanked the door open and fell in, right across Tracy's lap.

The next few moments disintegrated even further into farce.

Tracy and Brenda were yelling.

"Lee!"

"What's going on?"

I was yelling: "Back up and turn left!"

And we were all doing our yelling over the sound of some country singer wailing about drinkin', cheatin', and his mama.

I was sure everybody within a mile could hear us, but I didn't care. All I could think was that I wanted those girls out of there before the bad guys—the ones who had had guns when they invaded the Garretts' house—found them.

When I gasped out an explanation, of course, Brenda and Tracy—with the solid judgment of college-age youths—wanted to go up to the house. I thought I would have to throw myself in front of the car to stop them. It seemed like an hour before I convinced Brenda she should back up far enough to turn into the Double Diamond drive.

When we pulled up in front of the Double Diamond cottage, Alex Gold was standing on the porch.

"I was going to come after you," he said. "The nine-one-one operator still wants to talk to you."

I ran into the house and grabbed the phone.

"I'm sorry." I was gasping. "I realized that two tremendous—I mean, teenage! Two teenage girls were going to go up to the house any minute. I had to stop them."

"Don't leave again," the dispatcher said. "I have a unit headed for your address. How many intruders are there?"

I stood there, trying to give coherent answers. I was glad to see that Tracy and Brenda had followed me in. They were introducing themselves to Alex. I turned my back and tried to concentrate on the 911 operator's questions.

"I'm afraid they'll be gone by the time the patrol unit can get here," I said.

"What kind of vehicle were they driving?"

"I didn't see . . ." I gasped again. "I'll bet it was a blue Ford pickup. That's what they had this afternoon. And that's what the dead man was driving."

"Dead man? There's a dead man?"

"No! No! I mean the man who was found in the lake yesterday. I'm sorry I mentioned it."

The 911 operator was growing more and more confused, and she must have been ready to yell at me, but she kept her temper. She kept asking me questions, but my answers were getting more and more nonsensical. "Ask Underwood!" I said. "He knows who I am and how I fit in."

"Who's Underwood?"

I realized that I was talking to someone in the sheriff's office thirty miles away. She might well be unaware that Detective Underwood of the Michigan State Police was involved in an investigation at Warner Pier. The situation was way out of control.

At that point Alex tapped me on the shoulder. "I can see the lights of the police car," he said. "They're here."

"The police are here," I said. "I'm handicapped. I mean, hanging! I'm hanging up."

I slammed the receiver down and followed Alex out onto the porch. As I closed the screen door behind me, I realized he was alone out there. Brenda and Tracy weren't with him. I'd barely grasped that when Brenda's car started down the driveway.

"Where are the girls going?" I'm afraid I screamed the question.

"I don't know," Alex said. "When you said something about a blue pickup, they looked at each other and rushed out the door."

◆◆◆◆◆◆◆◆◆◆◆◆◆◆◆◆◆◆◆

CHOCOLATE BOOKS

Chocolate Without Guilt
by Terry Graedon and Kit Gruelle
(GRAEDON ENTERPRISES)

Terry Graedon is a medical anthropologist and coauthor—with her husband, Joe—of the "People's Pharmacy" newspaper column. Kit Gruelle is a pastry chef. Their credentials are impressive, and their goal is "recipes that taste decadent but can, with moderation, fit into a healthy diet."

People always put that moderation clause in, darn it.

But this small book—around a hundred pages, ringbound and most readily available through the "People's Pharmacy" column or Web site—opens with an overview of twenty-first-century research and scientific opinion on the risks and benefits of eating chocolate. This is followed by recipes for cookies, cakes, pies and tarts, frozen desserts, fancy desserts, and other treats. The nutritional content of each recipe is provided.

"Who'd guess that cocoa has more iron, ounce for ounce, than beef liver?" they write. But they also include a section on chocolate's hazards.

A simple, easy-to-understand look at chocolate and nutrition—plus recipes.

Chapter 17

I made a weak effort at running after Brenda's car, but I knew it was useless. After about thirty steps I stood stock-still in the Double Diamond drive, shaking my fists at the sky.

"So help me, God! If Brenda's still alive at midnight, I'm going to send her back to Texas, and then I'm going to fire Tracy's behind! I don't care if I have to personally watch the counter every hour we're open for the rest of the summer!"

Brenda's car turned south on Lake Shore Drive, just before a second patrol car went skidding into our drive. Neither car had used its siren, so I gathered some attempt was being made to catch the intruders in the act. But I doubted that they were still there.

The girls hadn't gone to the house. But where had they gone?

I went into the Garrett cottage and used the phone to call 911 again. I told the dispatcher that Brenda and Tracy had taken off and that I had no idea why, but I was afraid they were looking for the bad guys. I described both of them and pointed out that Brenda's car had Texas plates. The dispatcher didn't sound too excited, and maybe there was no reason to get excited. Knowing Brenda and Tracy, they might have simply gone off because one of them realized she was out of nail polish.

Then I called Joe on his cell phone. He answered on the second ring. I could hear Italian music, so I gathered that he, Pete, and Darrell had gone to the Dock Street Pizza Place. I guess I made sense when I tried to tell him what had happened. Anyway, he told me to stay at Double Diamond, and he'd be there in a few minutes.

Then I fell into one of the Double Diamond chairs, kicked off the flip-flops I'd borrowed, and rubbed my feet. "Uncle Alex—I mean, Mr. Gold! I'm sorry to have involved you in all this."

"Don't apologize! It sounds as if you got involved because you were a witness to the robbery over here."

"Maybe." I held up a flip-flop. "Anyway, thanks for lending me your beach shoes."

Alex looked at the sandals as if he'd never seen them before. "Those aren't mine," he said.

I looked at his tiny little foot, which was at least three inches shorter than mine. "I guess they belong to Dick then. If you don't mind, I'll keep them on until I get home."

He frowned for a moment. Then his face cleared. "You're welcome to them. You'd better wait here. Let the police handle things at your house. I'm sure they'll be over to talk to you in a few minutes."

He was right. Very shortly Warner Pier patrolman Jerry Cherry parked his patrol car outside and came to the door. Jerry's boss, of course, was my aunt's new husband, Hogan Jones. I'd known Jerry ever since I moved to Warner Pier, and I was glad he'd been the law officer detailed to babysit me.

No one had been found in our house, Jerry said.

"I wasn't imitating—I mean, imagining! I didn't imagine those two," I said.

"Oh, no. There are some signs of intruders. The other guys are checking for footprints and such, so you need to stay here until they're through."

"Is someone looking for the girls?"

"Oh, yeah. Detective Underwood got involved, and he sent a state police car south on Lake Shore Drive. And now, do you want to tell me just what happened?" Jerry smiled. "I know you told the dispatcher, but you'll have to tell it several more times."

Joe and Darrell came in while I was talking to Jerry. After Joe and I had held each other awhile, Joe said he'd walk over toward our house and see if he could find anything out. My impulse was to dig both hands into his shirt and pull hard to keep him from going, but I restrained myself. He instructed Darrell to stay at Double Diamond with me. Pete hadn't come in with them.

Shortly after Joe left, the girls came back. They'd gone about five miles south on Lake Shore Drive before a Michigan State Police trooper had pulled them over and ordered them to return to the scene.

I was still angry with them. "Why on earth did y'all take off?"

Tracy answered. "You said the guys might be driving a blue Ford pickup, and one had come flying out of Eighty-eighth Street as we came by. We thought we might see where it had gone."

"Of all the dumb—"

"Oh, Lee! We weren't going to stop it or anything. We just thought we might see where it turned off."

I bawled them out good and proper, but they didn't look contrite. "Well," Tracy said, "we didn't find it anyway. So I guess it was a waste of gasoline."

Joe came back in. "I almost got cornered by Harold and Alice," he said. "I told him you needed me here."

"I do."

"I guess Pete's around somewhere. I haven't seen him since we left the Dock Street."

In half an hour or so Underwood came in to quiz me. I explained how I'd come into the dark house and had seen the stranger at the front door, then a second stranger circling the house. Because one was tall and the other short, I'd decided that they might be the two men who had held us up at the Garretts'. Then I'd decided they were very likely the same two I'd stumbled over looking for Pete Falconer at the River Villa that afternoon. I told him how I'd fled down the basement stairs and escaped through the hole in the foundation, crawling out from under the current bathroom into the gaping hole that would eventually be covered by the floor of the bathroom addition.

The part that interested Underwood most was the angry comment I'd overheard once I was outside: "I'm going to bust Haney with an antique baseball bat over this."

I didn't know which guy had said it, but I was sure that was what he'd said. Underwood quizzed me several times to make sure.

"That's what it was," I said. "I didn't understand it then, and I don't understand it now."

"Is there anybody around here named Haney?"

"Not that I know of."

Joe didn't know of any Haneys in Warner Pier either. Even Tracy—who was likely to know everybody and everything about them—had not heard of anyone named Haney. We checked the Warner County phone book and found only one Haney listed, a John Haney who lived in Dorinda, the county seat.

"Why an 'antique' baseball bat?" Underwood asked. "Why not a regular one?"

I didn't have an answer to that either.

By then it was after eleven, and Underwood broke the news that we needed to stay out of the house until noon the next day so the crime scene team would be able to finish up in daylight.

"That's fine," I said. "If those guys are still on the loose, and it's too hot even to close the windows, I wouldn't stay in that house if it were guarded by a company of Marines."

"We'll go to my mom's," Joe said.

I glared at him. Was he forgetting our houseguests? "She hasn't got room for six people."

"It's either that or we drive thirty miles to Holland. You know we can't find rooms in Warner Pier. Not in July."

Brenda asked the key question. "Does your mom have air-conditioning, Joe?"

"Central."

Tracy, Brenda, and I spoke in unison. "Let's go."

Joe called his mom, and she agreed to take in the whole gang. Darrell hung his head and dragged his feet, but he obviously wouldn't find it convenient to stay in his camper while our house was overrun with crime scene investigators working thirty feet away.

So I laid down the law. "I'm sorry, Darrell, but you'll have to go along with the program. It's the best we can do. You'll probably have to sleep on the floor, so don't feel like you're getting any favors."

Pete still hadn't appeared. Joe wrote him a note and left it taped to our back door.

"I'm getting worried about Pete," I said. "Why hasn't he shown up?"

Joe laughed. "Pete is the last person to worry about. He can take care of himself."

We were allowed into the house long enough to pick up everybody's toothbrushes, and I got a pair of my own sandals. We arrived at Mercy Woodyard's house to find she'd lived up to her reputation for efficiency. She'd made up the double bed in her guest room for Joe and me, pulled out the folding couch in the den for the girls, and arranged for Darrell and Pete to stay with Mike Herrera.

Mike plays the dual role of the mayor of Warner Pier and Mercy's boyfriend. He has an apartment in a building he owns in downtown Warner Pier—the Sidewalk Café, which he owns, is on the first floor, Mike's business office and his catering operations are on the second, and his living quarters are on the third.

Mike had a guest room with twin beds, Mercy told us. She assured Darrell that, as a restaurant owner, Mike often took in employees who needed emergency housing. I'm not sure this was true, but it seemed to make Darrell feel better.

Joe drove Darrell over to Mike's apartment. When he came back he said Mike seemed pleased to help out, and Darrell seemed pleased that Mike also had central air-conditioning.

Joe tried to call Pete. His cell was out of service, but Joe left a message telling him he couldn't stay at our house and to go to Mike's.

He again told me there was no reason to worry about Pete. I decided he was right, or maybe I was simply too tired to worry about anything. We took showers and went to bed. I don't know that I slept terribly well, but I did sleep. I'd eaten breakfast the next morning before Mike called and said that Pete had never shown up to occupy the second twin bed.

Joe brushed off my concerns with a casual, "Oh, Pete can take care of himself." In fact, he was so casual I began to suspect he knew where Pete was. It wouldn't have been the first time Joe had kept some secret that Pete wanted kept.

I called TenHuis Chocolade to assure Dolly we were all right and tell her I'd be coming to work that afternoon, but that I'd have to wait until the crime scene folks let us back into the house, since I needed clean clothes. Especially shoes. The sandals I'd put on wouldn't do for work.

Then I helped Mercy clear the breakfast dishes. "I don't want to make you late to work," I said.

"It's hardly worth going in right now anyway."

"Is business slow?"

"I have lots of policies that are sold by the year, of course, so it's not as if I'm broke yet. But new business . . . it's been almost nonexistent this summer. Thanks to the Warner Pier grapevine."

"The burglary scare?"

Mercy nodded. "I guess it really infuriates me because it's so silly. First, there have been maybe twenty burglaries, and only half of them were my clients. Why am I getting the blame?"

"I know, Mercy. It's stupid."

"Besides, it's not like I have a list of the contents of people's houses. That's not the way it works."

"I think our policy just says 'house and contents.' Something like that."

"That's what almost everyone's policy says! People don't list their furniture piece by piece. If they list something separately, it's usually special jewelry. Maybe a sterling tea service. But who has things like that at Warner Pier?"

I handed Mercy a skillet and thought about that one. "There are lots of rich people around here. Don't they own valuable things?"

"Sure they do. But they don't usually bring them to their summer cottages. The antiques—now, that's

the problem. Because people do bring old furniture to
cottages. And if they leave it there long enough, it
becomes antique. But even most of those items aren't
particularly valuable. People don't usually list them
for their insurance policies. I don't have the slightest
idea what ninety percent of my clients own."

"What do you do if they make a claim?"

Mercy shrugged. "Take their word for it. It's nice
if they have photos or sales slips or some other kind
of record, but most people don't. It works most of the
time. But I couldn't tip a gang of burglars off to the
contents of my clients' houses. I don't *know* what they
have in their houses."

Mercy left for work, and Joe went out, saying he
was going to check in at the police station—one of
the benefits of being a city attorney—and he'd be back
to pick me up between eleven o'clock and noon.
"Keep the doors locked," he said as he went out.
"Don't open up unless you know who's there."

The girls were still sleeping, so I looked in the
drawer where I knew Mercy kept playing cards, found
a double deck, and dealt out a hand of Spider.

Of course, I couldn't concentrate on the cards. All
I could think about was that crazy chase the night
before. In my own house. Those guys had not been
plain old burglars. They had been lying in wait for
me. They had wanted to do me harm.

I was convinced that they had wanted to kill me.
Me. Lee McKinney Woodyard.

Apparently that was what Joe thought, too. Why
else would he have given me all the "keep the doors
locked" instructions?

But why would the baddies want to get rid of me?
Because I'd seen the two men in the boat? I hadn't
thought anything about them. I'd been looking for
Pete, not them. If they hadn't shown up in my front

yard, I would never haven given them another thought.

Did they think I might recognize them as the Double Diamond robbers? I hadn't. Until they came to the door.

And why did they come to the door? Our house had sat there all day with its windows wide open. If the tall guy and the short guy wanted to ambush me, why didn't they wait inside? Were they afraid that some other person—Joe or Pete or someone else they saw as more threatening—might walk in on them instead? Even the girls—if they'd beaten me home . . .

Waves of shudders went over me. I went to the den door and peeked at the girls, just to make sure both of them were breathing. The thought of the girls walking in on those two guys was going to give me the jimjams for a long time.

And what if I had parked in my regular parking place at the Baileys' house? I'd have had to walk down the path between the two houses. They could have ambushed me there. I'd never have had a chance to escape—through the Michigan basement or by any other route.

I thought about that possibility for a while. Then I called Joe's cell phone. He answered on the first ring. "Everything okay?"

"Yes. Everything's fine. I just got to thinking about those guys last night. They were waiting for me, Joe. They'd set an ambush."

"It sounds that way."

"But they could have broken into the house easily, and they hadn't. They weren't waiting inside. I wondered if they'd been waiting at the Baileys' house."

"Why would they do that?"

I went on without answering his question directly. "I simply forgot to park over there, the way I've been

doing. If they'd laid a trap for me at the Baileys' . . .
well, they would have gotten me."

"Lee, don't dwell on that sort of thing. Everything's
all right. You're safe. Try not to think about it."

"I'm not sitting here being morbid. I just wanted to
make sure that the crime scene people are checking
around the Baileys'."

He didn't answer, and I went on. "Because those
guys came up on the porch just about three minutes
after I turned on the lights in the house. That's just
about the length of time it would have taken them to
come from the Baileys' house to our house. And waiting for me over at the Baileys'—that would have given
them a better chance to catch me, if I had parked
where I usually do."

"But how would they know you usually parked
there?"

"From watching us, Joe. They would have been spying on our house."

I took a deep breath. "If the crime scene people
found as much as a footprint over there—even a cigarette butt or a hair—it would prove those guys had
been watching our house."

Joe took two deep breaths before he answered.
"You're right," he said. "It would prove *someone* had
been watching us. I'll check with Underwood and the
crime scene team."

Chapter 18

Mercy's house seemed cold and lonely after I hung up. I nearly turned the air-conditioning thermostat higher. Instead I pulled an afghan off the foot of Mercy's bed and wrapped up in it.

It wasn't that I'd forgotten how to enjoy air-conditioning. No, the thought of someone spying on our house had chilled me right to the bone.

If someone had been spying on us, who was it?

And why? Why would anyone do such a thing? Was it because Joe and I had witnessed the holdup at the Garretts' house? But Alex Gold had been a witness, and he seemed to be living a peaceful life. When I'd burst in on him the night before, he apparently had been sitting around enjoying his living room window unit. Why were we more threatening to the bad guys than he was?

Who? And why? I hadn't answered either of these questions when I heard someone stirring in the den. I peeked in the door and saw Tracy sitting on the edge of the bed. "Hi," I said. "Come on in the kitchen, and I'll trade breakfast for speculation."

That didn't exactly speed Tracy up, but in about

twenty minutes I had her sitting at the table with a Diet Coke. She's not a coffee drinker.

Tracy's eyes were still bleary, and she gave a broad yawn before she spoke. "What sort of speculation are you interested in?"

"Have you seen any strangers hanging around our house during the last . . . well, since you've been staying there?"

"Nope."

"Has anybody pumped you or Brenda about our little household?"

"Pumped me? You mean asked questions about who was staying there and why?"

"Yes. That sort of thing. Or maybe about who does the cooking or what do we do about laundry or just who all those cars belonged to and how we jammed all of them in the drive."

"I don't think so, Lee. Of course, Mr. Glick is always full of questions. But he's not a stranger."

"No, and he's lived there six months. I think this would be somebody new. I mainly wondered if you'd seen anybody you didn't know walking down our drive. Or on the Baileys' drive."

Tracy shook her head. "Sure haven't. Too bad Gina isn't here to ask."

"Gina?"

"Yes. She was always peeking out the upstairs windows, watching, if anybody went by."

"I hadn't realized that." I got up and raided Mercy's refrigerator for strawberry preserves, handing them to Tracy for her toast, but I was thinking about Gina.

Where had Gina gone? Why had she called the Holland motels trying to locate her ex-husband? And why had that ex-husband been using her dead brother's name? Why had that man—if it had been him—come to our house and asked for Joe, not for Gina? Was the dead man really her ex-husband? Was he one of the guys who had invaded Double Diamond and stolen the famous jewels?

Could the spy have been Gina? Was the spying connected to her disappearance? And where was Gina?

Was Gina dead?

My stomach got all fluttery. I'd worried about telling my stepmother that something had happened to Brenda. Now I began to worry about having to tell Grandma Ida that something had happened to Gina. Where could she be?

Tracy was speaking again. "Your house is sort of secluded, Lee. People don't wander by. As for strangers . . ." She snorted out a laugh. "It seems as if the people staying there are stranger than the people who walk by."

I smiled at her joke. Then I thought about it seriously. If there was a spy—and that was still an if, I reminded myself—could it be one of our group?

My emotions rejected the idea strenuously. I might get annoyed at being forced into the role of hostess for five people I didn't know well—even Brenda and I were practically strangers—but I had formed at least a slight emotional link to each of them. The thought of one of them spying on the rest of us was horrible, even worse than the thought of a stranger doing it. But I couldn't say it might not be possible.

Darrell? I felt sorry for Darrell. But pity didn't equate to trust. Darrell was hiding his thoughts and feelings. I didn't understand what was going on in his head.

And how about Pete? There was a mystery man if one had ever existed. He was definitely more than a bird-watcher. Could he have been telling the bad guys more than he shared with Joe?

Brenda and Tracy? They were simply too naive to

be deliberately revealing the details of how we lived. Of course, either might have let something slip to a person she trusted.

Which brought me to the boyfriends: Will Van-Klompen and Tracy's steady date, Jack Eberhardt. Had the girls told them about our ménage? Had some spy then asked the boys about the odd group where their girlfriends were staying?

All these things rolled around in my mind for an hour or more. Brenda got up, and she and Tracy watched some talk show in the den, but I was so taken with my own thoughts that I barely spoke to them. And after all that thought I came up with no new ideas.

After the jewelry had been hidden in Darrell's camper, I'd asked the neighbors if they'd seen any strangers around. Maybe something would still come of that. Hardly a revolutionary thought. But it kept me from thinking about the possibility that someone actually sharing our house had been telling the bad guys what we were up to.

I decided to follow up on my earlier inquiries. I bit the bullet and called Harold Glick. If anybody got around the neighborhood, he did. I was grateful when he didn't answer the phone. I left a message, saying I was still trying to figure out whether strangers had been prowling the neighborhood, and that I'd call him back.

I called several more people. Most of our neighbors weren't home, and the two who answered the phone didn't have any strangers to suggest. Both of them wanted me to tell them what had been going on over at our house. Having cop cars around doesn't enhance your reputation as a desirable neighbor.

My final call was to the Garretts. I'd found the number on my desk, where I'd put it the day Garnet came

by the office, and stuck it in my purse. Of course, I
knew that Uncle Alex was the only person at Double
Diamond, and I didn't think he would be any help.
But I called anyway. To my surprise, Garnet answered
the phone.

"Oh!" I said. "I thought you and Dick were in
Grand Rapids."

"We are. This is my cell phone number. Oh, Lee, I
talked to Uncle Alex this morning, and he told me
about the awful experience you had last night. I'm
so sorry!"

"Uncle Alex—I mean, Mr. Gold—saved my bacon,
or maybe my life. If he hadn't been home, I was going
to have to take to the woods. Barefoot."

"I hope, hope, *hope* that this had nothing to do with
our holdup. You and Joe must think we're interna-
tional spies or something."

She'd said the magic word. I interrupted her to ask
if they'd seen any strangers who might have been spying on our house.

"Everybody in Warner Pier is a stranger to me,"
Garnet said. "We're the newcomers." She gave a few
descriptions of people whom she'd seen walking down
Lake Shore Drive, and I quickly realized that my
quest was useless. A few of them I could identify. But
others . . . who knew? They could have been anybody.

"I guess I'm wasting time," I said. "A stranger
who's wearing a swimsuit could be renting a summer
cottage. Heck, in any neighborhood all a bad guy has
to do is paint 'Lawn Service' on the side of his pickup
and throw a power mower in the back. Then he can
go anyplace and do anything, no questions asked. I
guess we'd have to fall over somebody holding a tele-
scope up to his eye if we were going to identify a spy."

Garnet laughed. "I'm glad you can joke about it,
Lee. I'll talk to Dick; maybe he noticed someone."

"Whether he did or not, please tell him thanks for the loan of his beach shoes."

"Beach shoes? What beach shoes?"

"The ones he left by the door at the cottage. Last night I had to take to my heels barefoot, and my feet were already sore by the time I got to Double Diamond. So I borrowed a pair of flip-flops I found by the front door."

"Dick never wears flip-flops." Garnet lowered her voice. "He lost a toe to a lawn mower when he was just a kid. He's self-conscious about it. He always wears closed shoes. The flip-flops must belong to Uncle Alex."

"But Mr. Gold said they didn't. And they were much too large for his feet."

"Another mystery! Listen, I'll call you back if I think of anything."

We hung up, and I sat there idly wondering about the flip-flops. When Mercy's kitchen telephone rang I jumped. It was Joe.

"Listen, Lee," he said, "Underwood doesn't want us to move back into the house until he figures out who tried to kill you last night."

"Oh, gee! That's going to be real inconvenient."

"Yeah, but he's right. It's a lot safer. Mom will take us in."

"Have you asked your mom how she feels about this?"

"I called to warn her, and she said she was okay with it. Of course, we can't stay away from the house entirely."

"I hope not! I'm itching to get out there and get some clean clothes."

"Underwood says it's okay to go out there now. The crime scene team is just about to leave, and he's got a Warner Pier patrol car keeping an eye on things. Can you get a ride with the girls?"

"I'm sure I can. Aren't you coming? You need clean clothes, too."

"Maybe later."

I was catching a hint of excitement—or was it worry?—in his voice. "Joe, is something wrong?"

"I hope not." He took a deep breath. "It's Pete. He never has shown up. And now some farmer has called in and says a green SUV is in a ditch about five miles east of Warner Pier. Underwood's sending a car to check it out."

"You'd better stick with the state police, Joe. See what's going on."

"I'll call when I find anything out."

I arranged to pick up Darrell; then Brenda drove us all home. As warned, a Warner Pier patrol car was sitting in our drive. Plus, the mobile crime lab was still parked at the Baileys' house, and we could see glimpses of activity over there.

I was so curious I walked over to the Baileys' instead of going into my own house. The crime scene investigators, of course, waved me off, so I stood thirty feet away from the cement carport where I'd been parking and called to them.

"Have you found any sign that the bad guys waited for me over there?"

"Detective Sergeant Underwood will get a report."

So they weren't going to tell me anything. I watched them for a few minutes. One technician made a cast of something on the ground. Footprints or tire tracks? Another was looking through all the items under the carport. She had even taken everything out of the plastic bushel basket where Charlie Bailey kept the stuff he used when working in the yard. A foam rubber kneeler, a trowel, a pair of pruning shears, two nozzles for the garden hose, and a reel of plastic line for the weed whacker were all laid out neatly on the concrete floor. As I watched, the technician turned the basket upside down. Several sponges fell out.

I turned around and walked back to our house, frowning. Something about that basket bothered me. I didn't figure out what it was until I got home.

When I walked up onto the porch, a pair of black flip-flops were beside our front door.

That was what had been missing from the basket!

What were those flip-flops doing on our porch?

I realized that they were the shoes I'd worn back from Double Diamond at midnight the night before. I'd kicked them off on the porch before I went inside.

Dumb, dumb, dumb. I'd seen those black flip-flops sticking out of the top of that plastic garden basket every time I'd parked my van in the Baileys' carport. But when they disappeared, I hadn't missed them. When they reappeared—at Double Diamond—it had never occurred to me that they were the same shoes. Desperate for footwear, I'd simply put them on and worn them.

Now the question was, how did they get from the Baileys' house to Double Diamond?

And that wasn't hard to answer.

I went over to the Warner Pier patrol car and told our guard that I needed to walk over to the neighbor's house for a moment. The patrolman—a college student working for the summer—looked doubtful.

"You can come along," I said. "I want to be as cooperative as possible."

The student, who wore a name tag saying, SWARTZMAN, made a big deal out of calling in to say where we were going. Then he drove me down our road across Lake Shore Drive, and up to Double Diamond. He stopped outside the cottage.

He didn't accompany me to the door. I knocked and called out, "Mr. Gold!" After a bit of scurrying inside, Uncle Alex came to the door.

"Mr. Gold," I said, "I need to talk to Gina."

He batted his eyes innocently. "Gina? Gina who?"

"Gina Woodyard, my husband's aunt."

"Why would she be here, Mrs. Woodyard?"

"I'm not sure she is, now. But please don't tell me she wasn't here at one time."

He dropped his eyes and shuffled his feet. And I heard a giggle behind him.

"Oh, Lee, you found my hideout!"

Mr. Gold opened the door wider, and I saw Gina behind him.

Chapter 19

I was so glad to see Gina alive and whole that I resisted the temptation to wring her neck. I hugged it instead.

I then stood back and noted that she was wearing her pink high heels, the ones whose tracks I had followed down the drive.

"Gina, we've been so worried!"

"I'm sorry, hon. But I did call and say I was all right."

"That was before the murder!"

"Murder? What murder?"

For the first time I realized that Gina had no way of knowing that Joe and I thought her ex-husband was a murder victim. The Grand Rapids television and newspapers had mentioned that a body had been found in Lake Michigan and foul play was suspected, but no announcement had been made of my identification of the man as one who had claimed to be my husband's father. And no one had mentioned his bunion, the physical feature that he shared with one of the burglars. In fact, if any reporter had speculated about a connection between the robbery at

Double Diamond and the dead man, I hadn't seen the report.

Gina was frowning. "Was there a murder?" she said.

"Gina, do you have a photo of your ex-husband?"

She smiled ruefully. "Which one?"

"Art. Art Atkins."

"I might. I haven't cleaned out my wallet in a year. Why would you want to see a picture of *him*?"

"I'd like to see the picture before I explain."

She looked concerned, but went upstairs to get her purse without asking any more questions. As soon as she was gone, Alex Gold quizzed me about how I had figured out where Gina was. I explained about the shoes.

"I couldn't see how they'd gotten to Double Diamond unless Gina wore them over here," I said.

Alex Gold seemed quite proud of himself for giving her refuge. "Gina is a wonderful person," he said. "Of course, I've known her casually for years. But having a chance to become well acquainted with her has been a privilege."

I tried not to smile. Gina had made another conquest. Whatever "it" is, Gina definitely had it.

Gina came down with a big tote bag embellished with a sequined parrot. I felt like an idiot; I'd hadn't realized she'd taken her handbag when she ran away.

She pulled out a red leather wallet stuffed with papers. Then she sat down on the couch and began to pull things out. "Oh, I wondered where that receipt was. And here's my AARP card. And this picture— oh, it's my neighbor's son's graduation photo." She stacked money, scraps of paper, photos, membership cards, and credit cards on the couch in teetering piles, daring them to slip between the cushions. Finally, she triumphantly held up a small photo. "I knew I had one!"

She handed it over. Originally it had been a larger snapshot, and it had been cut down to fit into the wallet. It was creased and scarred, and it showed Gina sitting next to a handsome man in a restaurant or bar. I looked at it carefully.

The man was the same one who had come to the door and claimed to be Joe's dad, the man whose body was now in the county morgue.

"Gina, I have some bad news." I had no idea how she'd react to learning about Art Atkins's death.

She had seen the news coming. "Art is the dead man we heard about on television," she said.

"I'm sorry. I know you two had split, but once upon a time you must have cared deeply for him."

Tears were welling in Gina's eyes. "Art ran with a bad crowd," she said. "They wouldn't let him get away."

Uncle Alex reached over and patted her hand. She smiled at him. "Thanks, Alex. I'll be all right."

I tried to speak briskly. "You'll have to go and identify the body, Gina. And I'm sure the state police will want a statement. But can you explain a few things to me first?"

"I'll try, Lee. What do you want to know?"

I hardly knew where to start. "Just tell me about Art," I said. "And why you came to our house to hide out. And what made you take off so suddenly."

Gina sighed deeply and clasped her hands in her lap. "I never thought I'd wind up married to a burglar!" she said. "But that's what Art's profession was. Cat burglar! And he used me—*used me*—to locate victims."

"How did you find out about Art's . . . activities?"

Alex Gold seemed to turn pale. "Oh, Gina! They didn't use force!"

"Actually, no. That was what was so frightening. They didn't yell or threaten me. They spoke very softly, but they made it clear that if I called the police, they'd kill me. I'm not sure what words they used, but they got their meaning across. And after they could see I was scared enough to obey them, then they threatened Art."

"And you didn't want to see him hurt."

"No!" Gina pulled a handkerchief from the pile of things she'd unloaded from her purse. "I still had some feelings for him."

"Of course you did, Gina."

"They didn't believe me when I said I didn't know where Art had gone. They ended up by telling me I'd better find Art and tell him to contact Haney or we'd both be in a lot of trouble."

"Haney! Who is Haney?"

"I didn't know. I still don't know!"

"Had Art ever mentioned anyone named Haney?"

"Never. Honey, I was scared to death."

"Is that when you came over here?"

"No, first I wrote Art."

"I thought you didn't know where he was."

"I didn't. All I had was a Detroit box number. But I never got an answer. Then the two thugs came back. They threatened me again."

"Gina, you were really up a creek!"

"Yes, and not one paddle to help me out. All I could think to do was run away."

"So you came over here."

"As near as I could tell, the two thugs weren't watching me. So I drove over to Holland by a route so odd that I thought I would notice if someone was following me. I put the car in a garage and paid to leave it for a while. Then I took a cab to the Chevy dealership and called Joe. Bless his heart! He came right over and picked me up."

"Why didn't you tell us all of this, Gina?"

"I didn't want to get you involved."

I resisted the temptation to growl at her. She hid out in our house, but didn't want to get us involved. That made a terrific amount of sense.

Gina was speaking again. "Then you and Joe witnessed the robbery here at the Double Diamond cottage. And the next day I heard you telling Joe one of the robbers had worn jazz shoes!"

"Had Art worn shoes like that?"

"He hadn't worn them, but I'd seen an odd pair of shoes in his truck. I didn't know what they were. But when I heard you describe them to Joe, I knew that was what I'd seen." She leaned forward. "I nearly choked! You called to me to see if I was all right."

I nodded. "I remember. So you thought Art must have been involved in the robbery."

"Yes! And he did have a bunion. So I started trying to find him."

"You called all the motels in Holland."

"Did you hear me? I waited until you were in the shower."

"There are no secrets in that house, Gina. I overheard one of your calls. Did you find Art?"

"Yes! I mean, no! It was awful, Lee! Art was registered at one of the motels—as Andy Woodyard! When I asked to be connected to his room, one of those thugs answered! So I ran!"

"But, Gina, the thug couldn't have known where you were just from a phone call."

"But he did, Lee! As soon as he heard my voice, he began to laugh. It was a horrible sort of giggle.

And he called me by name. 'Well, Ms. Gina,' he said. 'So you didn't know where Art was, huh? We'll be out to your nephew's house to get you next!' "

She took a deep breath. "It was all I could do to answer him."

"He didn't come to the house looking for you. What on earth did you say to head him off?"

"I said, 'Oh, I'll be gone by the time you're here.' And I grabbed my purse and ran. I had an awful bad moment when I heard that little blond dog. I didn't want to run into one of the neighbors! But I hid behind the Baileys' house, and that fellow Harold didn't stop to see what the dog was barking at."

She looked at Alex Gold with melting eyes. "You had said that Alex was at Double Diamond, so I ran straight to him. And he saved me."

Alex Gold looked back with a gaze as melting as Gina's. He was obviously completely smitten.

Dyed hair, gaudy clothes and all—the woman was amazing.

Shaking my head, I went to the door and summoned the young patrolman. I introduced him to the missing aunt and told him she could identify the dead man. I added that she needed protection even more than I did. We waited at Double Diamond until he could call in and explain the situation to Underwood. Then we stayed until Underwood could send a patrol car to pick up Gina.

While we were waiting, I kept the phone busy. I called our house and told the girls what was going on. I instructed them to explain things to Darrell. I tried Joe's cell. It was turned off. I called the Warner Pier PD to try to find out about Pete's car. The department secretary answered and said she didn't know anything.

There was a lot going on.

As soon as a state police car arrived and took Gina

away, I went back to our house with the Warner Pier patrolman trailing along. I packed a bag for me and one for Joe, then checked the refrigerator, loading up the milk, lettuce, and lunch meat to take to Mercy's house. The temporary move was turning into a big mess. Even the thought of living in air-conditioning for a few days wasn't enticing. I wanted to be in my own place.

Darrell drove off in his truck with his belongings in the camper, something like a tortoise carrying his home along. He told me he was headed for Joe's boat shop. The girls were dawdling, of course, but I hollered up the stairs, urging them to finish up. I planned to take my own van this trip, but we'd help the patrolman if we were all ready to go at the same time.

While I was waiting, I did one last circuit of the downstairs, and when I looked at the screened-in porch I saw Pete's sleeping bag and canvas carryall piled out there.

Where was Pete? If we all left, the police wouldn't keep a continuous check on the house. Did Pete have anything that might be valuable?

How about his pistol?

I called Joe to ask his advice on what to do with his buddy's belongings. Joe's phone was still out of service. I'd have to use my own judgment. I squared my shoulders, went out onto the screened-in porch, opened the carryall, and began to look through Pete's stuff.

I was very pleased not to find the pistol. Pete must have taken it with him. It wasn't in my house, so it wasn't my responsibility.

Pete's camera was there, however, and his laptop. I stuck the camera into my purse and zipped the laptop into its carrying case. The girls finally came downstairs with their stuff, and we got into our respective vehicles and left.

I think the next two hours were the worst part of the whole thing. I wasn't being guarded, but I had to promise not to leave Mercy's house. Joe didn't call. Underwood didn't call. I was too distracted to read or watch television. All I could do was pace the floor and gnaw my fingernails.

When the phone finally rang, I could feel my heart lurch. I saw a familiar number on Mercy's caller ID, and I snatched up the receiver.

"Joe! What's going on?"

He sighed. "I have good news and bad news. And I hear you do, too."

"If you mean finding Gina. Yes, that was good. Have you seen her?"

He had seen Gina, but hadn't talked to her. I recapped her story as fast as possible. "So the good news is, she's safe," I said. "The bad news is that she might be charged as some sort of accomplice in these burglaries."

"If she tells everything she knows now, that probably won't happen."

"I hope not. Now, what's your news?"

"I'll start with the good. The state police have picked up the tall guy and the short guy."

"The ones who were at the house last night?"

"The ones we *think* were at the house last night. Anyway, they were in a blue truck registered as belonging to Art Atkins. Since Gina has identified the murder victim as Art, that's enough to hold them on right there."

"Good! Because I'm not sure I could swear they were the two in the house."

"You won't have to. They're also suspects in the disappearance of Pete."

"He hasn't turned up? But Pete's so . . . competent. It's hard to believe that something has happened to him."

"I know. I've been telling myself that since last night."

"And you said they found his SUV."

"They did. But there's no sign of him anywhere near it."

"No tracks or anything?"

"It's on a gravel road. Little possibility of tracks."

"Are they looking for this Haney?"

"Oh, yeah. There's one family named Haney in Warner County. The dad teaches English at Dorinda High, and the mom is a secretary at the Dorinda Reformed Church. The children are preschoolers. All of them have loads of alibis. That seems to be a dead end."

Joe and I were both quiet for a long time before I spoke. "Can I go to work?"

"It's probably all right. Just don't go roaming around, okay?"

"I'm not really dumb, Joe."

"I know. But you're real important to me. Until we know who this Haney is, don't take any chances."

We hung up, but I didn't feel a lot better. Where could Pete be? I'd found him a day earlier, but that had been a fluke—a deduction from one of his photographs.

Photographs! I realized that I had Pete's camera in my purse. If I looked at the photos stored in it, maybe I'd get a clue as to where Pete had been hanging out. Maybe there'd be some other place I could identify, someplace besides the River Villa with its distinctive red roof.

I dumped the contents of my purse out on the kitchen table and grabbed the camera.

Chapter 20

Until I got used to the darn camera, I thought I'd go blind. And even then, the tiny digital images didn't tell me a lot. Or perhaps, at first, they didn't tell me anything I hadn't already figured out.

Pete was definitely more than a bird-watcher. There were a lot more pictures of houses, of people, and of vehicles than of birds. And a lot of the photos were like the ones Pete had shown me earlier of the men on the beach—pictures he'd obviously taken surreptitiously. Whoever Pete was, he'd been spying on the people of Warner Pier.

There were all sorts of pictures of the tall guy and the short guy, the men I'd nicknamed Lofty and Shorty. They were pictured with the blue truck, with the white van, with their boat. But rarely was the background of the shots identifiable. It was simply a lot of trees, with a few water views tossed in. But I'd known that Pete had been watching the two men, so that wasn't new news.

The camera was loaded to capacity. I ran through dozens of pictures, and not one of them told me anything. Then I went back to zero and started over. This

time I paid attention to something I'd skimmed over
on the first view-through. There was a date and time
at the bottom of each picture.

I felt a jolt of surprise when I looked at the earliest
date and realized that Pete had been at our house for
less than a week. In fact, Darrell had been there only
two weeks, Tracy only ten days, and Gina only a week.
Brenda had been there a month, true, but it only
seemed as if we'd had houseguests forever. I shook
my head and went back to Pete's photos.

Looking at the pictures with the dates in mind, I
made a little more sense of the situation.

First, I found the pictures Pete had shown me earlier, the ones of the guys on the beach. When he'd first
shown them to me, I hadn't recognized them. Now I
realized that Pete had snapped the two guys casing
Double Diamond.

If he'd realized they were going to hold up the Garretts and had let Joe and me go to dinner there
anyway . . . he'd better stay disappeared, I thought.
Because when I got hold of him, I'd murder him. That
had been a darn frightening experience.

But I remembered that Pete had seemed concerned
and upset the night of the holdup, so I decided to give
him the benefit of the doubt. He had probably known
the two guys were up to something, but I couldn't
believe he'd known they were going to steal the Double Diamond jewels that evening. Surely he would
have done something about it.

Unless he was in it with them.

I stuffed that thought back into my subconscious
and continued to work slowly through the pictures,
looking at each one carefully. I found the ones that
showed the River Villa's red tile roof. Those were
close beside a set showing the ramshackle cottage

mer cottage into a year-round house. The friend's family sold their cottage. It was torn down, and a year-round house was built on that site. Aunt Nettie and Uncle Phil moved into the TenHuis cottage. They became friends with the new neighbor, who now owned the lilac bush that was a cousin of ours.

The new neighbor's name was Inez Deacon. Inez had moved to a retirement center a few years earlier, and her house was now occupied by—ta-da!—Harold Glick and his little dog, Alice.

Had Pete been spying on Harold Glick? Harold the lonely guy? Harold the dog lover? Harold the harmless pain in the neck?

I snorted. Impossible. We all avoided Harold as hard as we could. Oh, I felt sorry for him, but I didn't want to hang out with him. The idea of Pete the macho male keeping an eye on Harold's place was simply too silly.

But the lilac bush sure did look familiar. And there *was* an old shed on Inez's property, a barn of some sort. She hadn't used it in years, and it was barely visible from the road, at least in summer, because Inez's house was set in among a lot of trees and low, shrubby growth.

House on a busy street. Barn out of sight of the road. Actually, it sounded like the ideal layout for a burglary ring.

And that something blue. Surely it wasn't the truck Lofty and Shorty had been driving when they were arrested?

Ridiculous. It couldn't be.

But I reached for the phone. I'd turn the matter over to Detective Underwood of the Michigan State Police.

Or I would have if he'd been available. He'd been using the Warner Pier Police Station as his local headquarters, but again the only person there was the department's secretary. Everyone—including my husband—was out, she said. And Underwood was definitely unavailable. He'd gone to the state police facility south of Warner Pier to question Lofty and Shorty.

I told the secretary—I knew her, of course—that I had Pete's digital camera, and that it might help in the search for him. "I'll bring it by the station on my way to work," I said. "But I'm at Joe's mom's house if anyone wants it sooner." I didn't describe the lilac bush. The whole thing simply seemed too far-fetched.

The dispatcher assured me she'd tell either Joe or Underwood about the camera as soon as she could.

I hung up the phone, feeling virtuous, and began to get dressed for work. I admit that I was terribly curious about that lilac bush, but I would have resisted the temptation to take a look at it if I had had the right shoes.

One of the rules for working at TenHuis Chocolade is that rubber-soled, nonskid shoes must be worn by all employees. That's to avoid falls on the hard and occasionally slick floors of our commercial kitchen. Even though I spend most of my time sitting at a desk, I try not to bend the rules. I usually wear sandals or loafers, rather than the tennis shoes worn by the skilled workers who actually make the truffles and bonbons, but the soles of my shoes are of nonskid material.

When I'd picked up clothes at the house that morning, I'd grabbed up a shoe box with the name of my standard work loafers on the end. That box, I now discovered, did not contain my standard work loafers. It held a pair of high-heeled sandals I'd taken on my honeymoon, a honeymoon that had actually included a Broadway show. Joe and I had taken a taxi from

the hotel to dinner and another from dinner to the
theater. Comfort hadn't mattered; glamour had. The
shoes had a higher heel than even Gina ever thought
about, and I'd had to clutch Joe's arm with every step
I took. He hadn't complained.

I hate to admit it, but when I opened that shoe box,
a thrill passed through my body. I could not possibly
wear those shoes to work, and neither could I wear
the slippery sandals I'd stepped into earlier.

I was forced to run by the house and get another
pair of shoes.

That meant I could drive down the interstate for
another mile, take a different exit, and approach our
house from the south, not from the north, as I usually did.

That route would give me a look at Inez Deacon's
lilac bush.

I would not have to stop the car or do anything
remotely dangerous. But I might actually be able to
identify that lilac bush and give Underwood a strong
suggestion of a place he might look for our missing
man, Pete.

There would be no danger at all, I thought smugly.

I was in the van in less than the time it takes Dolly
Jolly to roll a tablespoon of nougat into the filling for
a truffle. I flipped on the air-conditioning and headed
for the interstate. Just a mile past my usual exit, I
turned onto One Hundredth Street. A mile west of
that exit I came to Lake Shore Drive and turned
north, headed toward home at a leisurely pace that
gave me plenty of opportunity to examine the local
flora, such as lilac bushes.

I went past the minimansions that had sprung up
south of our hundred-year-old farmhouse in the past
few years, mentally admiring some and criticizing others while I decried what they were doing to our prop-

erty taxes. I passed the Veranda Bed-and-Breakfast, with its private elevator to the beach. I went by what had once been the Lally House, a largely glass structure now renamed Lakeview, and looked away. Not only had I once had a bad experience there, it was also the place where Joe was introduced to his first wife. We tended not to talk about that house.

Now I was getting near the curve, and just around it was Inez's house—now rented to Harold Glick. Because of the curve, the side yard of the house was visible from Lake Shore Drive, or it would have been if there hadn't been so many bushes. But could I see the big lilac? Or the barn?

I slowed down. And I looked.

And, yes, back in the woods, there was the big lilac. And beyond it, barely visible because it was July and the woods were fully leafed out, was the old barn.

And coming out of a small window in the side of the barn was an arm waving a white cloth.

An arm waving a white cloth?

I nearly drove by without stopping, so astonished that I couldn't figure out how to hit the brakes.

Then I knew—simply knew—that it had to be a signal, and I stood that van right on its nose.

Who could be signaling from the barn of a man I suspected of being part of the burglary ring?

It had to be Pete.

I pulled off onto the narrow gravel shoulder along Lake Shore Drive, and I jumped out and beat my way through the woods, picking my way around evergreens and maples and through blackberry bushes and probably poison ivy toward the window where that white cloth had been waving.

Now I could see that the window's glass had been knocked out. Ugly shards were still sticking up in the top of the frame, and more glass was on the ground outside.

I stood on my tiptoes and peeked into the window. And I saw the prematurely gray hair and eagle-beak nose of Pete Falconer.

Pete was leaning against the wall with his eyes closed, and at that moment his arm and the white rag were hanging limply. For a wild moment I was afraid he was dead. Then I remembered that his arm had been waving only a few minutes before, and he was still upright.

"Pete?"

He opened his eyes. "Lee! Thank God! You can go for help."

"Are you locked in?"

"Yes! And I think I broke my damn leg chasing your crooks."

"I'll get you out!"

"No! Just go to a safe phone and call the cops. Tell them Harold Glick is George Haney! They can take it from there."

I heard a creaking noise coming from the other side of the barn. "What's that?"

Pete's voice became a hiss. "He's back! Run!"

He disappeared from the window.

I decided running would make too much noise. So I ducked. I squatted down under the window and stayed as motionless as I could.

I heard noises inside the barn—thumps and bumps. Then I heard a low, ominous chuckle. "Tried to get out the window, huh?" It was Howard Glick's voice. "A lot of good it did you." I heard a thud and a deep groan. It was easy to picture Howard kicking Pete.

The bastard.

Harold gave another chuckle. "You haven't got too

much more time, you dirty cop. I'll be back with the gasoline in a few minutes, and that's when the barn's going to burn down."

I heard more movement inside the barn, and a trickle of sweat began to run down my forehead. Then another ran down my back. A third down my side. Trickles became tickles. I longed to rub the sweat away, to scratch. But I stayed still.

Then the thumps and bumps were farther away. A creak sounded. It was the same noise I'd heard earlier, and I figured out that it came from a door on the other side of the barn. Was Harold leaving the barn? I heard Alice begin to bark, and I deduced that he had left and had walked up to his house.

Staying on all fours, I crawled to the corner of the barn. I could see the house. And I saw Harold. I dropped to my stomach. He was putting two gas cans in the truck of his gray Chevy. He slammed the trunk lid and opened the driver's-side door. Alice jumped inside, and Harold got in with her. He started the motor and drove away.

As soon as he disappeared, I was on my feet. I circled the barn. It had only one opening large enough for Pete's giant frame to pass through. That was the door. It was locked with a padlock.

I could handle a padlock.

But it wouldn't take Harold more than twenty minutes to get to the nearest gas station, fill his gas cans, and get back.

I ran through the woods, back to Lake Shore Drive and my van. I jumped in, started it up, and drove around to Harold's drive as fast as I dared. I backed into the drive and up to the barn door. Then I popped the rear hatch, yanked open the compartment that held the spare, and took out the jack handle. In three minutes I had pried that padlock off the door, hasp and all.

When the door creaked open, I saw that the only thing I could see in the barn was a U-Haul truck.

"Pete!" I went past the truck to the broken window. Pete was lying under it.

"Lee! I thought you went for help!"

"I'm not leaving without you. Glick may come back before the cops can get here." I knelt beside Pete. His right leg was swollen until it filled the entire leg of the camouflage-patterned pants he wore. His bare foot stuck out the bottom, the size of a ham. His condition made me feel sick.

But we didn't have time for pity. I tried to make my voice firm. "Can you stand up at all?"

"I don't know."

"Try." I made it an order. Pete hauled himself up by grabbing the frame of the window, and I helped by boosting him. Then, using me as a crutch, he hopped toward the door. Getting him that twenty feet wasn't easy for me, but it must have been agony for him. He ground his teeth with every step, but he kept going.

When we got to my van, I slapped the spare's compartment down, and Pete slid himself into the rear deck. For once I cursed the training I'd had from my mechanic father, training that meant I never leave junk in my car. There wasn't a blanket, a raincoat, or even a sweater in there to help Pete be even slightly comfortable. I ran around to the driver's side and reached in for a bottle of water. I'd drunk part of it, but when I tossed it to Pete he snatched at it like . . . well, like a guy who hadn't had a drink in twenty-four hours.

I reached up to close the van's hatch, but Pete spoke before I could.

"Blue pillowcase," he said. "U-Haul. If you can, get it."

I slammed the hatch, then ran back to the U-Haul. Sure enough, in the front seat there was a blue-and-white striped pillowcase. I grabbed it up.

And I couldn't resist taking a peek.

Inside I saw colors and shapes that I'd never seen before. Chains, serpents, bugs, flowers. Squares, diamonds, circles. Reds, blues, greens, golds.

I was holding the Diamonte collection.

I don't know if the knowledge scared me, or if it simply distracted me. Anyway, as I came out of the barn I caught my foot in those darn blackberries. Down I went.

For a moment I didn't know if I was hurt or not. And by the time I realized I wasn't, something wet was rubbing my face.

"Darn you, Alice!" I said. "Stop it!"

The silly little blond mutt was delighted to see me.

I was terrified to see her, of course. If Alice was there, so was Harold.

Chapter 21

I got up, with Alice underfoot, and I tried to cover the few feet to the front of my van. It was like a wrestling match. Alice was frisking around so enthusiastically that I could barely walk.

"Git! Alice, git! Scoot! Scram!"

Alice didn't get the picture. She wanted to be friends.

I tried to step over her, but suddenly I heard a voice. Harold Glick's voice.

"Alice! Alice, you dumb mutt! Come!"

Alice began to bark in reply. She grabbed my pants leg and worried it. She yipped. She yapped. She chased my toes. She jumped on me.

I was trying to make progress toward the van, and I was trying to hold on to that pillowcase.

"Alice!" Glick's voice was louder. "What have you got?"

I had almost reached the driver's side when Glick came around the corner of his house. He was no more than forty feet away. He had a clear view of me. And he had a clear view of that blue striped pillowcase.

He roared.

The driver's-side door was still standing open. I jumped inside. And so—damn it!—did Alice. I ignored her. I slammed the door, locked the doors, turned the key, and threw gravel getting under way. Harold jumped aside as I squeezed the van between his car and his house. I tore out onto Lake Shore Drive, headed toward town.

Alice was leaping from the backseat to the front. But she didn't block my view of Glick as he came out onto Lake Shore Drive after me. He was holding a pistol.

"Pete! Get down!"

The back window shattered, but Alice's yapping kept me from hearing the sound of his shot.

Harold Glick! Shooting at us! Hiding the loot from the Double Diamond holdup in his shed!

Now it seemed so obvious. But I would never have guessed that dull, boring Harold was part of a burglary ring. Even his claim to have been the first burglary victim had been a ploy—a ploy to make him look innocent. And he'd lied to me about seeing Gina get into Art's white van. And he'd lied about hearing people running up Lake Shore Drive the night of the robbery at the Garretts' house. And he'd undoubtedly been the person who planted a piece of the stolen jewelry in Darrell's camper.

Not that I had time to think about Harold's sins at that moment. No, I was headed for town with a badly injured man in the back of my van, with a museum-quality collection of Art Deco jewelry in the seat beside me, with the back window shattered by a gunshot, and with a darn dog leaping all around and barking like mad.

Alice was making so much noise I could barely hear Pete yell. "Why'd you bring the damn dog?"

"She came on her own. I'll have to get into Warner Pier before I can stop. If I go to the house, Glick will follow us."

"Sure." The word was a groan. "I've held on this long. I'll make it a little longer."

It's only ten minutes from our neighborhood to downtown Warner Pier, if you don't hit a traffic jam.

It may sound stupid to talk about a traffic jam in a town of 2,500. But in July Warner Pier becomes a town of 25,000 that still has streets built to accommodate the traffic of a town of 2,500. Those narrow streets are among the features that make us such a quaint little Victorian town; a feature that helps draw the 22,500 tourists who drop by every week in summer to keep our local businesses afloat.

I believe each of those 22,500 tourists was driving in a separate car that day. I've never seen such traffic.

As soon as we reached the bridge over the Warner River, the bridge that links our semirural part of town with the main, historic section, I reached for my purse, ready to pull out my phone now that we should have service.

But Alice—darn her!—had another idea. She snatched my purse away from me, and she pulled it through the gap between the two captain's chairs in the front seat of the van.

"Alice! Give me that!"

Alice was having a great time. First she was loose in a van to jump around all she wanted, and now she had this wonderful playtoy made of leather with a fun strap to chew. She shook the purse all around and growled at it.

When I hit the first stoplight—the one at the end of the bridge—I turned around to take it away from her.

Alice didn't like that. She let me get hold of one

corner; then she bit her sharp little teeth into my wrist. When I let go, she grabbed the purse by the bottom and flipped it end over end.

I watched in horror as my cell phone flew out and went under the backseat.

"Oh, Pete! That dog has thrown my cell phone under the seat. Can you reach it?"

I could hear how desperate I sounded, but Pete only moaned.

"Pete! Pete? Pete, are you all right?"

His answer was impossible to understand.

The cell phone was a lost cause, the traffic was a nightmare, and Alice was still dancing around in the backseat. Then she was looking out the side window, paws on the door, nose pressed to the glass. She paused for a second, perked her ears up, then started barking more madly than ever.

I looked. And in the gray Chevy beside me, just pulling up even, was Harold Glick.

He'd caught up with us.

But prayers are answered. My lane suddenly began to move, and I moved with it. I gunned the motor and got into the passing lane—headed the wrong direction—to get around a slow-moving car. I drew ahead. Now, if I could just get to the police station. And if there was someone there to help me. The police department secretary wasn't going to be a lot of help.

I put my hand on the horn and held it there. I waved cars out of my way. I played chicken with tourists whose hair must have turned white on the spot. But Harold hadn't caught up with me when I hit Peach Street. And there was Warner Pier City Hall, with the police department in the rear of the building.

And there were three parking places beside it.

That might sound good, but it wasn't. Each of those

places was marked OFFICIAL POLICE VEHICLES ONLY. If all three were empty, that meant no cops were in the station. Pete and I would be no better off there than we were already.

I turned into the alley behind the police station. I might not be able to go to the station, but I had to get off the downtown streets, clogged with tourists' vehicles.

I tore down that alley, knocking one Dumpster galley-west. I barely paused at Fourth Avenue, sneaking across through a hole in traffic that shouldn't have let a bicycle through. Now my horn wasn't the only one blasting. I scooted up the alley toward my goal, the only parking place I could count on finding in all of Warner Pier: my own reserved place behind Ten-Huis Chocolade.

I cut into it so quickly that I could feel my rear tires lose their traction and go skidding three feet left of where I wanted them to be.

"Pete! I'll get help!"

I grabbed my keys, then reached for the pillowcase that held the jewels.

And I heard a car roaring toward me.

It was Glick! He was coming down the alley at me.

I'll never know how I got to the back door of Ten-Huis Chocolade. I had it open, then slammed and locked behind me before I even knew what I was doing. I was in the TenHuis break room, and Dolly Jolly was staring at me, amazed.

I didn't give her any explanation. I just jumped for the phone on the wall and hit 911. I let my explanation to the dispatcher explain things to Dolly. I could only hope Pete was all right; it would take too long to get him out of the van.

Dolly caught on right away, jumping to her feet. "I'll lock the front door," she said, and she headed toward the front of the shop, through our big, clean commercial kitchen.

Luckily, the break room phone had a long cord. I moved enough to watch her go toward the front.

She was too late.

Through the plate-glass window I saw Harold's car stop in front of the shop. Harold didn't give a darn about traffic; he just jumped out and ran for the door. He had it open before Dolly could get halfway through the kitchen. He rushed through the shop—Tracy stood at the counter staring—and he was headed for me.

What could I do?

I dropped the phone, moved five feet into the kitchen, and lifted the lid on the closest chocolate kettle, one that held 250 pounds of melted milk chocolate.

And I upended the pillowcase that held the jewels. Every last beautiful, historic, valuable piece went inside and began to churn around with the paddles that kept the chocolate smooth and liquid.

Then I defiantly faced Harold Glick and yelled at him, "You can't get it!"

Harold roared and raised his pistol. I ducked behind the vat. Then I heard him scream.

I looked out to see him wrestling with Darrell.

Darrell had come out of our front storeroom—the one where we had wanted him to build more shelves. He'd come up behind Harold, and he'd swung his arm around Harold's neck.

Caught completely by surprise, Harold was losing his footing, but he still had his pistol.

As I watched, Brenda and Tracy darted in from the shop. Brenda rushed into the storeroom behind the two struggling figures. When she rushed out—not more than a second later—she held a hammer. Darrell's hammer. "Hold him still, Darrell!"

Brenda whacked his elbow with that hammer. Harold screamed, and he lost his hold on the pistol.

Darrell threw Harold down onto the floor, and he, Tracy, Brenda, and Dolly all fell on him, one on each limb.

Alice ran up and licked his face.

Chapter 22

The next hour was a mishmash of ambulances, police cars, friends, relations, and one little blond mutt who tried to help as Dolly and I emptied 250 pounds of melted milk chocolate from its kettle and cleaned the Diamonte collection with hot, soapy water.

Things were so wild I don't think I really understood just what had happened until I saw pictures of Gina and Mercy on the eleven-o'clock news a day and a half later.

"These two brave women—sisters-in-law—hired a private detective at their own expense and worked with Michigan State Police to break a major burglary ring that had specialized in valuable antiques," the newsanchor said. "A Warner Pier man police think is the leader of the ring was arrested Friday afternoon. Authorities believe he killed one of his fellow burglars and also seriously injured a Detroit private detective, Peter Falconer."

Joe and I were watching the news in our own living room. Alone.

"So," I said, "Pete is a private eye."

"Right."

"But you told me you'd once represented him. Back when you were a defense attorney."

"That was true, but it wasn't a criminal case. It was the only divorce I ever did. Apparently I didn't do a very good job. Pete came out of the experience with a profound distrust of women."

"I noticed that. How did you meet Pete?"

"He did investigations for the agency I worked for in Detroit. He's a former cop."

The television newsman was talking again.

"A truck loaded with valuable antiques was discovered in a barn on property leased by Harold Glick, who a state police spokesman said is actually George Haney, a convicted fence. Also being held are two men authorities believe were members of the ring, John Tallboy and Kurt Small."

"Tallboy and Small!" I said. "Surely those aren't the names of Lofty and Shorty!"

Joe laughed. "Yes, they are. However, Tallboy is the short guy, and Small is the tall one."

We laughed. The reporter listed Art as the dead man, and reported that Falconer was being treated for an injured leg at Holland Hospital. Then the report on the burglary ring bust was over, and I clicked the remote to turn the television off.

In less than forty-eight hours our lives had turned over, and possibly the most revolutionary change was that all our houseguests had left.

Gina had collected her car from the Holland garage where it had been stored and rushed home, ready to calm any fears Grandma Ida had developed over the news reports.

Darrell had heard of a permanent job as a carpenter in Detroit and had left to try to land it. I'd also learned from Joe that Darrell was waiting for a major financial settlement for unlawful imprisonment. He wanted to be easy to find when his money came through.

Tracy's parents heard of our excitement and rushed back to Warner Pier to check on their only daughter. She'd moved home, and Brenda had gone to stay with her for a couple of days.

Pete was in the hospital, facing surgery the next morning. Joe had been by to see him that afternoon.

Alice had been given a new home by a Warner Pier animal lover.

So Joe and I were alone in the TenHuis cottage. It seemed strange.

"Joe," I said, "people keep talking as if a burglary ring just happened to be established right in our neighborhood and that that ring just happened to include your aunt's husband. Coincidences happen, but that's not logical."

"No, Underwood believes it began with Gina—or maybe with Grandma Ida."

"What could Grandma Ida have to do with a burglary ring?"

"You know how excited she was when she learned that Aunt Nettie's house was across the road from Double Diamond? She told everyone about it—including her son-in-law, Art Atkins. Underwood thinks that was the germ of the plot to steal the Diamonte collection."

"I thought it was when Art married Gina."

"That was the other germ. But you're right. It was no coincidence. That's what Gina had figured out. And that's why she was in enough danger that she ran—twice."

"Let's look at it chronologically."

"Maybe that's the best way. First Gina met Art. They fell for each other—or she fell for him—and

Gina's the type who wants things legal. But Art had already had a long and successful career as a burglar— I call it successful because he had no convictions. And one reason he'd been successful was that he had always worked alone. But even a lone burglar has to have a fence. So he had hooked up with George Haney."

"The guy we knew as Harold, the dullest guy on the lakeshore."

"Later, yes."

"I talked to Gina, Joe, and she's convinced that Art really cared for her, that he was killed because he wanted to protect her."

"There may be elements of truth in that. Harold needed Art's expertise on antiques for the burglary gang he organized. And Lofty and Shorty say one reason Art was killed was that Harold became convinced he was hiding Gina. And Art must have been looking for Gina; at least, I can't figure out any other reason for him to come by our house and make that crazy claim that he was my dad. He must have thought you'd tell Gina."

"Maybe if I had, if they'd gotten together, then Art wouldn't have been killed."

"We'll never know. But let's remember that Art began by exploiting Gina's knowledge."

"So how did this lead to Harold Glick becoming our neighbor? Was it just because Warner Pier is a place with lots of wealthy families who own summer cottages—and antiques?"

"No, Underwood thinks Harold came because of the Diamonte collection."

"But Harold moved over here six months ago, and the Garretts and the Golds hadn't been at their cottage in years. How would anyone know that the collection would be making a stop here?"

"They read it in the *Chicago Tribune*."

"Oh, come on! I read about the exhibit of the collection in the *Trib*, but it didn't say anything about Warner Pier."

"You didn't read the article with the attitude of a thief, Lee. Underwood got hold of a copy this afternoon, and the story said that the Chicago show was a final exhibit of the collection as a whole, because it was to be auctioned off. Alex Gold was even quoted as saying the family was going to have a reunion so each member could select a piece to keep as a souvenir. Elsewhere in the article it mentioned the family's longtime ties to Chicago and that they had a summer cottage on Lake Michigan."

"That's still a far-fetched deduction."

"It gave Art a direction to steer Gina, and she was able to pick up gossip—quite innocently—and learn that the Garretts and Alex Gold were going to take over their summer cottage again and were planning to hold a family reunion there this summer."

"Oh. So if anyone knew about Alex's habit of carrying valuables . . ."

"Right. And Gina says lots of people in the antique business knew that Alex carried jewelry that way. In fact, Underwood told me plenty of jewelers carry valuables casually, just stick them in their pockets. They feel—maybe rightly—that it's safer to do that than to make a big deal out of it."

"Because a special bag or a bodyguard would attract attention."

"That's the idea. Anyway, six months ago Harold found a house to rent that was within walking distance of Double Diamond. And it had a handy-dandy barn for storing the gang's loot from other burglaries."

"I wonder if I mentioned that house to Gina."

"Don't worry about it. Harold had a plan that would have worked with any house he rented. He had definitely made the move from fence to become leader of the burglary ring. After he moved over here, he claimed to have been the victim of the burglars, assuming that would make him look innocent. Then all he had to do was walk Alice around the neighborhood every day, keeping an eye on the Double Diamond cottage until he saw it had been opened."

"Meanwhile," I said, "Lofty and Shorty had rented that ramshackle house up the river and were making themselves and their boat part of the scenery."

"Right. Art hung back until he was needed. As I said, Art always liked to work alone. But he was definitely committed to the theft of the Diamonte collection, and he was going to need to fence the stones through Harold."

"Then Gina figured out that Art was a thief and, even worse, that he'd been pumping her for information about potential victims."

Joe nodded. "She pleaded with him, asked him to give up crime. Of course, she was talking to a guy who'd never earned an honest dollar in his life, so she didn't have much of a chance at changing him. When she figured that out, she filed for divorce. Art took off."

"Poor Gina," I said. "Harold was looking for Art, so she was threatened by Lofty and Shorty."

"That was when she called me and asked if I knew a private investigator. She was desperate to find Art, and she knew both of them were in danger."

"And you didn't tell me!"

"I didn't know, Lee. All Gina told me was that she had some problem with her husband. I thought she was trying to catch him with another woman or to find hidden assets. It never occurred to me that he was a burglar! Luckily, I recommended Pete, and he does have experience in undercover criminal investigation."

"How did your mom get involved with Pete?"

"About a month ago she realized that the rumors about the burglaries were affecting her agency. So she asked me about a private detective, too. By then I knew that Pete was looking into the burglaries, though I didn't know he was doing it for Gina. So I suggested Mom call him. Pete saw the connection right away and began working with the insurance companies."

"How did Darrell fit in?"

"Only on the periphery. Pete was one of the group who had worked to get Darrell released. Those guys were still keeping an eye on him, making sure he had a place to live and wasn't too lonely. So Pete pumped Darrell for prison gossip about Haney—Harold—when he was trying to find Art. Darrell was eager to return the favors Pete had done for him and asked more questions than he should have. That had two results. First, he heard that Tallboy and Small—Lofty and Shorty—were looking for Art. Second, Lofty and Shorty heard that Darrell had been asking questions, and all of a sudden Detroit was too hot for Darrell."

"So that's why you suddenly decided you needed a helper for the summer."

"Pete called me, Lee. I couldn't say no. But at that time it didn't occur to me or to Pete that the burglary gang was already in place—right in our backyard."

"How did Pete get hurt? I never have understood that."

Joe laughed. "He fell out of the loft in Harold's barn. He'll never live it down."

"What was he doing in the loft of Harold's barn?"

"When you called us away from our pizza to tell us that Lofty and Shorty had been lying in wait for you at the house, Pete, Darrell, and I all took off at top speed. But Pete already had ID'd Harold as George Haney, though he hadn't seen fit to share that information with any of us. So while Darrell and I went to make sure you were okay, Pete went to Harold's to see if Lofty and Shorty had gone there. They had. The three of them were talking in the barn, and when they drove off, Harold left the door standing ajar. Pete couldn't resist. He slid inside to see what was there."

"And he found the U-Haul truck."

"Right. It hadn't been loaded then. Harold came back, and good old athletic Pete hid by climbing into the rafters. Unfortunately, one rafter wouldn't hold him. It broke, and he tumbled down right at Harold's feet."

"Pete had his pistol! Or, at least, it wasn't in his stuff on the porch. I'm surprised he didn't plug Harold."

"Pete apparently managed to land on his head and his leg at the same time. He was unconscious after the fall."

"He probably landed on his leg and banged his head on the truck."

"That's more logical. Pete thinks he was out cold for at least fifteen or twenty minutes. When he came to, Harold had taken his pistol and locked him in."

"He apparently intended to kill Pete. Why didn't he do it then? Lofty and Shorty are claiming Harold stabbed Art, right? So he's cold-blooded enough to kill."

"Right. But it was easy to dispose of Art's body. He was killed in the boat, so they stripped his burglar outfit off and threw him in the river. Pete was different. Harold couldn't leave until the next day, so he would have been stuck with a dead body for twelve to eighteen hours, and he didn't know if Pete had told anybody where he was going. Pete was smart enough to pretend to be unconscious or groggy whenever Harold came around."

"And Harold didn't think Pete could get out of the barn."

"If Pete had been in tip-top shape, he could have gotten out. He would have kicked the doors and popped that padlock right off. But with only a window too small to get out and just one usable leg . . ." Joe shrugged. "You definitely saved his life, Lee."

"Pete told me to go call the police, but when I heard Harold say he was going for gasoline . . ." I shuddered. "It's not far to the Shell station. I thought we had only ten or fifteen minutes to get him out."

Joe pulled me close. "I love you," he said.

"I love you, too, Joe." I kissed him on the ear. "And I want to remind you that Brenda will be back the day after tomorrow."

"I'm aware of that, and I have a surprise for you."

Joe took me by the hand and led me into the bedroom. In an inconspicuous corner behind the dresser was a machine I'd never seen before.

"It's a present from Pete," he said. "A little thank-you for saving his life."

"What is it?"

"It's a portable air conditioner. You can use it in any room without installing it."

"Turn it on! Quick!"

The air conditioner works great. Or it did for a few hours. At two a.m. the next morning a cold front came through. The lakeshore temperatures dropped into the low fifties, and we didn't need an air conditioner the rest of the summer.

About the Author

JoAnna Carl is the pseudonym of a multipublished mystery writer. She spent more than twenty-five years in the newspaper business, working as a reporter, feature writer, editor, and columnist. She holds a degree in journalism from the University of Oklahoma and also studied in the OU Professional Writing Program. She lives in Oklahoma but spends much of each summer at a cottage on Lake Michigan near several communities similar to the fictional town of Warner Pier. She may be reached through her Web site at www.joannacarl.com.

Chocoholic Mysteries by
JoAnna Carl

EACH BOOK INCLUDES YUMMY CHOCOLATE TRIVIA!

Looking for a fresh start, divorcée
Lee McKinney moves back to Michigan to work
for her aunt's chocolate business—and finds that
her new job offers plenty of murderous treats.

THE CHOCOLATE CAT CAPER

THE CHOCOLATE BEAR BURGLARY

THE CHOCOLATE FROG FRAME-UP

THE CHOCOLATE PUPPY PUZZLE

THE CHOCOLATE BRIDAL BASH

Available wherever books are sold or at penguin.com

"I began to hear about these burglaries, and they were happening to people I knew. Or at least knew about."

She turned to Alex Gold. "Art was an antique finder, you know. At least, that's what he told me. He never had a shop, though sometimes he'd help in mine, and he was very knowledgeable about the field. Mainly he cruised around, looking at estate sales and tag sales. He'd be gone a week or more, and when he came back, he'd have a panel truck full of tables, dishes—small items. We were careful to keep our businesses separate. If he had costume jewelry or china or something else I might be able to sell, I'd pay him for it. His prices were quite reasonable. I thought he was giving me preferential treatment! Then I got a flyer from the Michigan Antique Dealers. They described a tea service that had been stolen in Grosse Pointe. I nearly fainted. I had it in the shop at that moment, and Art had brought it to me.

"Then I thought back, and I realized that a lot of the places that had been burglarized were places I'd visited or heard of, then had discussed with Art."

"What did you do?"

"I'm not shy! As soon as Art came home, I confronted him! And he didn't even deny it. He just laughed and said, 'What you didn't know didn't hurt you.' I was furious."

I reached for Gina's hand. "I'm so sorry, Gina."

"I told him our marriage was over. I said he'd have to get out."

"How did he react?"

"Oh, with sweet talk. He promised to reform, to keep his business legitimate. That time."

"That time?"

Gina smiled sadly. "Of course, he didn't mean it. I

found that out fast enough. A month later I found more questionable goods stashed in the back of his van."

"The white van with the orange sign on the door."

"Yes, that belonged to Art. Plus, he had a blue Ford pickup he used sometimes." Gina sighed. "I rummaged around and discovered that he had three sets of magnetic signs for that van! And he had extra license plates for it, too! Then I found a driver's license with Art's picture, but Andy's name and birth date!"

I nodded. "He'd raided the family records."

"I see now that I'd almost encouraged him to do it. I'd told him all about Andy being drowned, and, well, I think he pumped Mama. He was really nice to her, took her out to lunch, things like that. Mama had always said Art had the Atkins mouth. He was a third cousin, you know. But it never occurred to me that he'd steal Andy's identity!

"When I found that driver's license, I told Art it was all over. For good. That was two months ago."

"Did he leave your house?"

"Yes. Not that he'd been there much anyway. But he packed his stuff up—including the things I thought were stolen—and moved out. I knew I should go to the police, but somehow I couldn't. I filed for divorce. I thought that was the end of it."

"What happened next?"

"Some . . . well, I can only call them thugs . . . These two thugs showed up looking for Art. They came right in the house, looked all around. I was scared to death."

"Did you call the police?"

"I threatened to do that. That's when the party got rough."

where I'd seen Lofty and Shorty. Their boat was clearly visible.

I kept looking at pictures. Pete actually had taken lots of bird pictures, and some of them were amazingly good. But the bird pictures were interspersed among what I was calling the "spy" pictures.

But what I needed to know was where the photos had been taken, and I wasn't picking up many clues about that. Some had been taken at the cottage on the river, and some at the beach. I knew that the state police were aware of Pete's interest in the ramshackle cottage on the river—I'd told them myself about seeing the two guys there, and they'd actually arrested them. So I felt confident that they'd searched that area looking for Pete. And Pete obviously wasn't at the Beech Tree Public Access Area. It was a public beach, for heaven's sake.

I was discouraged, but I kept looking at the pictures. I'd have to call Underwood and give him the camera. Maybe the state police would have somebody with X-ray eyes, someone who could decipher the pictures and link them to their location. And maybe if they did, it still wouldn't help. Pete could be anyplace.

It wasn't until I came to the final three pictures—pictures that were dated only the day before—that I got a clue, a clue in the form of a lilac bush.

It wasn't blooming, of course. Lilacs bloom in the spring, not at midsummer. But I still recognized it, mainly because of its similarity to our own lilac bush, a huge thing that practically engulfs the east side of our garage.

The lilac in Pete's photo was as large as ours, probably twelve feet high and twenty feet wide. It wasn't all one bush, of course. It had spread in the long years since it had been planted. The lower part was thin,

with flimsy little branches and stems that looked as if
they didn't get enough sun, but the upper and outer
branches were full of graceful leaves, oval at the top
and pointed at the bottom. They'd always reminded
me of the symbol for a spade on a deck of cards.

In the first picture, Pete had focused the camera on
a cardinal's nest in the lilac bush. The mother cardinal
had been sitting on her eggs, and she was so well
camouflaged that I almost didn't see her. In the second
photo, her nest was out of focus. At first I thought
Pete had simply goofed, had taken a bad photo.

Then I realized the focus had been on something in
the background. Something blue. He'd been using the
lilac bush for cover while he took a picture of something a long way behind it.

Something blue. Unfortunately, I could see only a
corner of the blue object. I couldn't tell what it was.
And what was the dilapidated building behind it? The
third picture showed more of the building.

On my first run-through I had thought that the ramshackle building was merely the one where I'd seen
Lofty and Shorty. But the lilac bush had told me
different.

That was a lilac bush I knew personally.

Or was it? On second thought, I wasn't sure.

The family story—passed on years ago by Uncle
Phil—is that my great-grandmother planted our lilac
bush back when the TenHuis cottage was a brand-new
summer place. At the same time, she gave a lilac bush
to a friend who had a cottage a little way south on
Lake Shore Drive. They had a friendly rivalry over
their lilacs. Every spring they took snapshots of them,
measured them, and compared whose bush had the
most glorious blooms.

Time went by. My great-grandmother and her friend
both died. My grandfather turned the TenHuis sum-

front of the vent. She looked as if she were going to cry. "I'm afraid so," she shouted. "And they swore they had it fixed yesterday."

Dolly is a food professional who had come to work for TenHuis Chocolade a year and a half earlier and who had taken to the chocolate business with the ease of a kid biting the ears off an Easter bunny. Dolly is even taller than I am and is broader, too. She has brilliant red hair and a face to match. With Aunt Nettie abroad, Dolly and I were in charge.

"Have you called Vandemann?" I said.

"No!" Dolly speaks out at a shout. "I'm afraid the young guy can't handle it!"

"I'll try to get hold of Mrs. Vandemann. His mom runs the business side." I held up my hand, offering Dolly support as she climbed down from her precarious perch.

"We'll have to move stock around!" she yelled.

The skilled chocolate crew, the wonderful women I call the "hairnet ladies," were already beginning to move boxes of chocolate and racks of bonbons into the front half of the big kitchen. Having our air-conditioning out wasn't just an inconvenience. It could shut us down completely.

TenHuis Chocolade is completely air conditioned, of course. It has to be. Heat and humidity are the enemies of fine chocolate. People say, "I'm melting," when it gets hot and humid. That's just a metaphor. But it's a fact for chocolate. A bonbon—or any other kind of high-quality chocolate—will get soft at eighty degrees and will actually lose its shape at ninety.

And high-quality chocolate is expensive. The finished product is expensive, and the ingredients used in it—chocolate, sugar, cream, butter, flavorings, and fondant—are expensive. Heat and humidity can ruin all of them except the flavorings. So a heat wave is a potential disaster for a chocolate company, and problems with the air-conditioning are a guaranteed disaster.

TenHuis Chocolade has three separate air-conditioning systems. One cools our retail shop and my office, and two cool the big workroom, the storage rooms, and the break room. If even one of them goes out, it's a problem. But now, faced with a terrible heat wave, both the work-area AC systems had been acting up.

"Did you turn it off and on?" I said. Sometimes that helps.

Dolly nodded. "I tried! No use!"

I shook my head and headed for the telephone. I had Vandemann's air-conditioning on my speed dial, and I put in a panic call to Mrs. Vandemann. I pointed out that her son had worked on our AC only the day before, and hinted that if he couldn't fix it, we'd appreciate his recommending someone who could.

We try to patronize local businesses, but there is a limit.

Mrs. Vandemann made soothing noises and assured me her son would be there immediately. Or almost immediately. He was fighting a similar emergency at the Warner Pier twenty-four-hour clinic, she said.

I refused to be intimidated by sick people. They could live with fans; my chocolate couldn't. I hung up, then reported Mrs. Vandemann's assurances to Dolly, who was standing in my door.

"But I'm going to call Barbara down at the bank," I said. "First, if worse comes to worst, and we have to replace that unit, we'll need credit. Second, she may recommend some other air-conditioning company."

Dolly frowned. "I hate for you to have to bother with this, Lee, when you have so many other problems."